The Truth Is in Here

Peter John Ravlich

The Truth Is in Here
© 2014, Peter John Ravlich
ISBN 978-0-473-29116-7

Paperback Edition 1.0, June 2014

Published by inklings.co.nz
Contact peter@inklings.co.nz

*Dedicated to Claire and Ralph, whose relationship
and soundtrack continue to inspire and amaze us all.*

CONTENTS

01 - HOW DO THEY WORK?

I carry a pocketful of magnets. The little alphabet ones are good, and you can pick them up at the pound store for, well, a pound; but you get twenty-six of them. The store attendants get suspicious if you buy too many sets, but I find two or three are plenty every other month or so.

If you like, you can take a screwdriver and pry the actual magnets out from their plastic casings, being careful of your fingers; but I quite like the effect of the letters: they don't hurt, and add a dash of colour. They aren't the strongest magnets, won't wipe your cards or magnetise your keys, but they do a beautiful job.

They also add a nice distraction when passing time, as you can slip a hand into your pocket and manipulate the little magnetic fields, feeling them attract and repel one another.

So why the magnets, you ask? Or maybe you don't. Maybe you're already one of us. I won't claim to be the first, or the most committed. Maybe you're already an enlightened citizen, an economic vigilante, or maybe you just hate parking operators. Either way, the magnets help me to facilitate one of my daily good deeds and acts of rebellion.

Have you seen them at work, parking wardens? They glide down the rows of parked cars, endlessly alert for timely transgressions, waiting to pounce. Those sharks of the sidewalk are as merciless as any of nature's predators, but carry an unnatural glee that prances across their faces in the instant of preparing a ticket.

Have you seen a parking warden's face, in contrast, when you take a colourful magnet from your pocket, and affix a used but still-valid parking ticket to the front of the ticket machine with a satisfying little clunk?

Or perhaps you've seen the face of the next driver who parks nearby, fumbles for change in her glove-box, curses her way to the machine, and there discovers the pre-paid ticket, waiting just for her.

She gets a tiny victory, a small thrill of satisfaction, and saves a pound or two. She may even keep the magnet and pay the favour forward. More important, though, is the direct hit on the profit margins of Big Parking, an industry rarely surpassed in evil.

It's not just about parking, of course: the magnets work equally well for any ticket-based scam, and I'm sure you can think of a dozen other appropriate uses.

Like most of my daily activism, it's more about education than money. If I can remind one random stranger about our culture of indiscriminate waste and profiteering, my day is a little brighter. If I can make a parking warden scowl, so much the better.

I'm Martin, by the way, did I forget to mention that? You don't need my surname, because this isn't about me.

02 - THE WATER COOLER

They call us conspiracy theorists, but we're really just trying to live without hypocrisy, at least as well as any human can.

They teach the young that history is written by the victors. But then they disregard their own words, treat them as so many other rote facts, and continue, divorced from that crucial and critical context.

We are the ones who remember. Who fail the tests and refuse to drink the Kool-Aid. We trust what we can see, what we can experience. That means relying on our senses, which can mislead us, and our minds, which can distort or forget: but these are all we really, demonstrably, have, and at least we acknowledge our limitations.

It can be difficult, balancing a modern career with an honest life. I learned the hard way that a finance office is not the best place to chat about the unbound greed that drives our economy.

People have been taught not to rock the boat. "Life isn't fair" has become an excuse rather than an observation, a deft phrase to avoid anything uncomfortable, anything challenging. A reason not to try.

You're still listening, though, so I'm sure you're not one of the drones. If you feel any lingering discomfort, you should probably stop now, and go back to your life. This isn't all playful magnets and mind games. It's going to get a lot harder, a lot messier, and it's only for people who are ready to know the truth, to experience it for themselves.

For far too long, I worked as a temp. I managed to subvert my disgust at office culture by treating it as a rigged game, a chance to observe from within the systems I ultimately hoped to bring down. That helped me not to get too invested, too ashamed of my own participation in the machine. That, and I needed the money.

Of course, the water-cooler provided an outlet, a pressure-valve letting me release the odd spurt of critical thought.

"Martin! Did you catch the game on the weekend?"

"Hey Sam, what game?"

"The football. You watched it, right?"

"No, sorry. I don't follow any sports, as a matter of principle."

"Sounds like an odd principle. Any sports? What about rugby?"

"Nope, don't follow that either. Institutional sports are the modern equivalent of religion: a panacea for the masses."

"A pana-what-now? How about golf?"

"Spectator sports are a carefully orchestrated ploy to absorb leisure time and provide an outlet for suppressed middle-class rage."

"I..."

"Hear me out, Sam. It's different if you play the sport yourself - if you're an avid footballer, then watching is a way to appreciate a common skill-set and critique your own performance in contrast - but watching without physical investment is just a way to vicariously join the privileged few and stoke artificial patriotism."

"Here's one you can agree with: beach volleyball. Every guy loves watching beach volleyball, am I right?"

"Beach volleyball is even worse! It manages to add hyper-sexualisation and objectification of the players of either sex to the mix. It's truly a symptom of where our culture has been directed that we're subjected to such spectacles."

"But... boobs."

"My point exactly. Sport is a distraction from the real concerns of the world. Wave some admittedly well-sculpted abs or generously-proportioned cleavage at the screen, and you give the viewers the perfect excuse to avoid thinking. There might be no visible harm, but it's time and energy that you could invest in a more productive or noble pursuit. I'm all for satisfying physical desires, but sports and other spectacles are crafted to make them the sole focus of our lives.

"Sculpture, music, art, love: the very foundations of civilisation are at our fingertips, but we end up far more interested in this week's playoffs than developing our talents, or having any real say in how the country is governed."

"Er, is that the time? I've got a meeting in five, Martin, catch you later."

Such encounters let me pass on the odd bit of authentic thought, but few seemed too interested in second or third conversations.

Even viewed as a game, office work wasn't quite what I expected. I would arrive at 8am, shuffle papers and try to look busy until 11, then head off with the other temps for an early lunch. The work seemed to consist of circular email discussions, endless committee meetings, and a lot of gossip.

I had expected days of doctoring transactions, followed by hushed conversations and even quieter threats: everyone knew that the corporate world ran on blackmail and closed-door relationships. But the Old Boys' Club was evidently closed to us lower echelons, giving a veneer of legitimacy to the organisation.

Outside the office, I had my photography. A valuable respite from the drab corporate world, it provided a connection to purity, untempered by human excess or corruption.

That's if you disregard the ugly supply chains and sweat-shops of the global manufacturing behemoth, but I tried to choose my subjects to highlight such contradictions beneath the art.

Tweaking a composition to capture the perfect shot, watching the play of light and shadow and deciding where to shoot, or even cleaning my equipment, all of my rage and concern about the world would fade away, along with everything else. Everything, that is, except for her.

03 - ORGANIC MATTERS

"Okay, let's go over this again." She stood wrapped in a sodden towel, hair still dripping from the shower.

"I don't want to talk about it, love, can't we go and eat?" It was shaping up to be one of *those* evenings. I slumped on the couch, trying not to be distracted by her state of undress, and failing.

"Not until I talk some sense into you. Just answer the question: have you ever sat near the wings on a plane?" She disappeared into the bathroom as she spoke, and returned with a second towel - my towel - wrapped around her hair.

"Fine. Yes, I have." I inhaled the lavender scent of her shower lotion and conditioner, trying to remain calm, in control. It wasn't working.

"And have you looked out at the air, flowing over the wings?" She somehow managed to look sarcastic even while drying off and selecting clothes.

"Obviously, yes."

"Have you noticed the way you can see the air, pooling around the front of the wing surface?"

"Um, yeah, I suppose so."

Her eyebrows arched slightly, as she prepared to pounce. "Well, that's what we call condensed air, dear, and it forms a vapour trail."

"You don't have to patronise me. How do you know that's what it is?"

"Because it's demonstrable, according to your own 'seeing is believing' garbage: you see the vapour forming over the front of the wing, and no indication of nozzles or any other odd devices, and this vapour, at the very low temperatures outside the plane, streams out behind in a shaped mist or fog."

"That doesn't mean the plane isn't *also* dropping chemicals."

"No, but you have no possible reason to postulate that it is: the visible trails left behind by the plane are the apparent result of the wing and engine vapour, and you can't say that just because a conspiracy is possible it is necessarily true."

She continued, before I could even start to formulate a reply, "The thing to remember about verified conspiracies is that there is *always* a whistleblower. After fifty-plus years of contrail paranoia, don't you think there would have been a single person overcome by conscience if there was anything to it? For God's sake, you get a dozen ex-military types confessing to UFO involvement each year, but not a single claim that anyone was involved in this ridiculous plane theory. What do you think these supposed chemtrails do, anyway?"

"There are boundless possibilities..." I grasped for one. "Cancer has been on the rise for decades..."

"Now that's just offensive, Martin, and you're not that stupid. Cancer diagnoses have been on the rise because people are more aware of it, more likely to get screened. People are also living longer, making them generally more prone to diseases associated with cellular division and aging. You don't need to search the closet for monsters when you know there's a branch tapping on the window."

"I don't want to argue with you."

"Because you can't." She was dressed now, somehow able to handle both intense discussion and practical tasks simultaneously. For some reason, this display of competence really bugged me.

"No, I'm just hungry and tired, and don't want to fight. A lot of people believe in chemtrails, there must be a reason."

"Doesn't that make you one of the 'sheeple' you rage about? More people think it's a load of crap, if you want to take the democratic approach."

"Fine, I think we'll agree to disagree on the matter."

"No, we'll agree that you were wrong. Now let's go get some food. I'll let you pay, by way of apology."

"Thank you dear, you're all heart."

She can be frustrating, and we often differ slightly in opinion, but God I love her.

04 - MECHANICS 101

The terminals outside were busy with the bustle of any international airport, and the air hung thick with dust. The hangar was quieter, almost still in the afternoon heat. Two figures scampered around beneath the fuselage of the Boeing 737 that occupied the building, their frames dwarfed by the massive aircraft.

"Hand me that spanner, will you, Roy?"

"Sure thing - the shifter?"

"Do you see another spanner?" His hand idly stroked the waiting nut, marking it for his attention.

"Here you are, smartarse. Hey Phil, I've been thinking."

"That's trouble." His fingers fractionally tightened the thread of the spanner around the nut, before he gently torqued it.

"I'm serious. I've been wondering why we do this?"

"Why do we do what? We've all got to eat, pay the bills."
Phil grunted a curse as the spanner slipped from his grease-lined grasp, rattling down to the concrete floor. He stooped to retrieve it, careful not to bump his head on the fuselage, as Roy continued speaking.

"Nah, I mean, why we need these systems at all. There have got to be easier ways to distribute chemicals. Are you telling me that in over a century, nobody's come up with a better method?"

He took a deep breath and finished tightening the nut before her replied - second time lucky. "It's the same old story: business as usual. Of course there would be better ways by now, but some big firm would have the patents on them. Going old-school might need a few more chemicals, but keeps the lawyers away."

"Sorry I asked. I mean, the fact that we do this at all is a better-guarded secret than the Colonel's fifteen herbs and spices, so who's going to sue us?"

"Eleven herbs and spices, and you'd be surprised. Most of the big players keep eyes on the competition, if you know what I mean."

"I'm not following."

"Spies! You've gotta know what the rest of the field is doing- you'd be stupid not to."

"Now you're being paranoid. Didn't you hear what they did to Atsu? He arranged a meeting with a journo, and bang! Have you got that third tank hooked up yet? The connection looks a bit wonky from here."

"Still need to tighten that clamp - almost there. What do you mean, 'bang'?"

"I mean they shot him. Found his body in Soho, I heard, they pinned it on a prostitute."

"Poor bastard. What was he thinking, going to the press?"

"Way I hear it, that's the funny part - it wasn't anything to do with the work, after all. His kid had won some swimming trophy, they were doing a story on her training regime."

"Bad luck, then, but he should have cleared it with them upstairs. At least the girl will have his redundancy. Should pay for a few classes."

"Some consolation. I wish they wouldn't call it that: 'redundancy,' it's a pretty shitty euphemism. Call it blood money, I say. You nearly done? It's too hot to keep this mask on for much longer."

"Yeah, but think what it's protecting you from. Don't want to breathe this stuff."

"What does it do, anyway?"

"What does what do? The chemicals?"

"Yeah, the chemicals... We hook them up, maintain the systems, and we know we're not supposed to inhale them - but what are they?"

"Above our pay grade, buddy - just be glad we're almost done for the day."

"I sometimes wonder if it's just a ritual, a placebo, these days. Giving the punters what they expect."

"I sometimes wonder if you think too much. Don't want to get Atsued."

"Too soon, man. He was one of ours, even if I didn't know him well. Could have been me, or you."

"My bad, but keep your head down, stop yapping so much, and you'll be fine. Let's get the nozzles checked; I've got half a sandwich waiting in the hangar."

05 - COINCIDENCE, IF YOU BELIEVE IN THAT SORT OF THING

You're probably wondering how we met. Actually, you're probably wondering something completely different, but let's pretend that's where you were going with the thought.

It doesn't have as much of a stigma as it used to: we met in a brothel.

I mean online.

Let me rephrase that: we were both playing an online game, and our in-game avatars met in a brothel underneath a tavern. I'm sure it goes without saying, but we were there to complete a quest. I was, anyway.

We got to talking, and quickly discovered that we had very little in common. Remarkably little, really, given that we were playing the same game. That made us talk more, discussing our points of difference until the small hours of the morning.

I failed the quest, for the record, but got a date. I left the brothel in high spirits (I'm not certain whether that part is normal or not) and spent the next week preparing myself.

Online meetings are rife with deception. It's kind of implicit when you're talking through a pink-haired, large-breasted, hermaphroditic gnome mage, and she's an Ent-like bardic tree-creature. How do you transport those otherworldly impressions to the physical realm? Add in a dash of desire, and you've got a recipe for awkwardness and disappointment.

Bracing myself for this was a large part of my preparation. Eventually, though, the time passed. I ironed a shirt, found some clean jeans, and managed to get there without incident.

I sat waiting in a local café. You may stop me here, quite correctly, and ask whether it was truly a *local* café. Most right-minded people abhor the spectre of Starbucks and other cancerous tendrils that encroach on cottage industries, especially when they do so beneath laughable banners of "fair trade."

I had, of course, done my homework, vetting the café through the Companies House: Only two directors listed, both with local addresses.

I'm not stupid, though, and companies often register subsidiaries and franchises with the appearance of local enterprise, so I checked out the shareholders, too. They were also local, with low online profiles, and no indicated trappings of wealth or success.

I'm not an entirely trusting person, so I then took an extensive look at reviews of the café. All were dismal, in the two to three star range, which confirmed a legitimate local business: The big chains pour money into viral marketing, buy reviews, and threaten sites who give them poor ratings. I'll take a good honest two-star eatery over a five any day.

Unable to do much more with the resources at my disposal, I confirmed the café for our meeting.

Local business or not, café remained a misnomer. It's near-impossible to get a decent coffee in London. Hazelnut-flavoured syrup with burnt shots of coffee-like gunk serves as the most popular stand-in, and most stores sport an array of "organic" juices, made by the same companies who enzymatically engineer corn-syrups for higher fructose yields – but little in the way of well-roasted, freshly-ground, perfectly-extracted bliss-in-a-cup.

I sipped tea, instead, and tried to guess what a tree creature would look like in person. My own appearance is decidedly male and human, with brown hair and a sprinkling of "natural grey highlights," according to my barber.

Two cups of orange pekoe later, I was beginning to suspect that a tree creature owned neither watch nor cellphone.

Then in she stumbled.

Love at first sight may be one of the biggest clichés of the cinema century, and wasn't a fair description in this case: this was love at first fall.

How could you fail to lose your heart to a girl who skipped through the door, tripped on the stoop and collapsed to the ground in a physics-defying sprawl? She appeared to have an extra dozen limbs, judging by the flurry of flailing as she drifted downward, and they each grabbed at my heart as her vertical drop continued in slow motion.

I'd like to say that I dived forward and caught her in a single fluid action. I'd like to say that I followed the heroics with a witty one-liner, guaranteed to snare her heart.

What happened, though, was not quite so text-book. I sat frozen in my chair, mouth open in amazement. Then I laughed. I laughed loudly enough to drown out the thump as the girl of my dreams met the solid wooden floor.

Please let me explain: I'm not a tosser. Well, I might be, but that's not why I laughed.

I had always been sceptical of romanticism, considering it nothing more than a coordinated hoax at best, a pipe-dream perpetuated by Hollywood.

I had dated, of course, explored my sexuality and bedroom preferences, grown through that teenage longing for the latest sanitised ideal, and come to some sort of terms with my desires.

Until that moment, I had thought I was cool: a sexually mature individual, with refined and realistic expectations.

Then she appeared, and I was hit with a fluttering in my chest and hormones threatening to leap from my body. I thought a little giggle was warranted.

She didn't.

She picked herself up off the ground (ignoring my extended hand) and spoke her first words to me through a scowl: "I hope to hell you're not Martin."

Our conversation improved from there, at least enough that I secured a second, more successful, date.

They say that the rest is history, but that's cheating it, more than a little. The rest was life, a life I hadn't asked for or deserved. A life with her.

Within two weeks we had agreed never to get married. Within three we were moving in together. Sometimes, everything falls into place. Our story just took that more literally than most.

I should mention someone else at this point, or I'll forget. Just a little over nine months after that first date, little Barnaby arrived in our lives.

I say "arrived," and it's accurate, but misleading.

We went for a look, and returned with a dog. Or the papers for one, anyway.

We picked him out ourselves, after we watched him fighting his litter-mates for food. He was the runt of the pack then, an uncoordinated scrapper with something to prove, and Shelley said he reminded her of someone – she never did say who.

The RSPCA delivered him to our apartment the next day, all de-wormed and vaccinated.

A few months on, and he was a little larger than we'd anticipated. And still he grew. He's a big, lumbering mongrel of a dog, but he's our big lumbering mongrel, and we love him.

06 - BETTER NOT TO ASK

I said earlier that this isn't about me. That might not have been strictly true, but it's not an autobiography. Every human journey is unique, and the only way I can really initiate you is to open a window into my discoveries so far, to give you a glimpse through my eyes, a context for my actions and beliefs.

I've been asked, at times, how I got so paranoid. The question is full of indoctrinated bias, but the essence is worth covering: this is how I started questioning the world around me.

I should mention here that I didn't grow up in London, nor in the nominally United Kingdom. Where I started out can sit with my surname in the relative safety of silence. I'm something of a nomad, I suppose, like so many inhabitants of London, victim to the gravitational pull of its absolute *placeness*.

(London isn't exactly the greatest location for anyone concerned with privacy, but I didn't learn that until after I arrived, and leaving might have appeared suspicious: so there I remained.)

As a child, I remember discovering children's books on the unexplained, tucked away in the non-fiction section of the school library. These beautiful volumes introduced me to early friends such as Nessie, The Bermuda Triangle, poltergeists, psychics and the mysteries of ancient Egypt.

Such research captivated and amazed me, imparting a real sense of mystery: proof-positive that the world would always have unfathomable depths. The comfort that offered to a young boy was immeasurable, if short-lived.

Tragedy never struck, in the Hollywood sense, but slowly imposed itself on my reality.

The first warning sign was my mother's response to these discoveries. I wanted to share my newfound knowledge with my family, yet she was strangely dismissive from the start. She was sceptical even of phenomena that seemed consistent with her stated religious beliefs, which genuinely confused that naive little boy.

 I didn't know it at the time, but that was my first experience of parental hypocrisy, and even unnamed, I hated it. Those stilted, difficult conversations helped to found my quest for truth, but it was a couple of years before a third-party set me more fully on the road.

The person in question was my science teacher, and the fateful conversation was conducted in front of my classmates.

"How about you, Martin, have you decided on your science project?"

"Yes, sir. I plan to conduct an experiment on food preservation."

"Okay, and what hypothesis are you testing?"

"I'm going to investigate the preservative properties of pyramids, using cardboard replicas of various pyramid configurations and bacterial cultures. I'll compare the growth rates of the cultures within different pyramids, along with controls in a standard cube and the open air."

"Ah, so you're positing that the shape of the pyramids will focus the cosmic rays to stop the bacteria from growing?

Or are you counting on sacred geometries? Listen carefully, class, Martin is some kind of wizard."

"Um."

"Don't be shy, boy. Go on, tell us all about your magical theory."

"Er, it's not my theory, sir - I've read some books..."

"I'm sure you have, Martin, but this is a science class, and we're talking about a science project, and I'd appreciate it if you'd choose a topic that involved actual science."

So, I've just realised that my science teacher was kind of an arse. If I'd been less naive, I probably would have been scarred by that discussion, but it just opened my eyes at the time. If you couldn't trust books vetted by the school librarians, who the hell could you trust?

The reaction of my classmates was also illuminating, if sad. They laughed at the science teacher's taunts, but didn't really care. I don't mean that in a callous sense: they didn't care that there was no way of knowing, as a student, which books held truth and which fiction or speculation. And that's where I parted philosophical company from my peers.

I didn't get in many playground fights at school, but I do remember one. Our health teacher had introduced the benefits of vaccination as the bedrock of modern Western medical systems, which had led to a slight altercation.

I mentioned the Tuskegee syphilis experiment, and pointed out that many modern medical processes are built in response to horrendous violations of human decency, and that advocating a shining beacon built on exploitation and corruption was hardly a positive model for developing nations. Then we got started on the drug companies.

It turned out, funnily enough, that the father of a classmate was one of the faceless executives at a pharmaceutical multinational.

Maybe calling them drug-dealers was a little too colourful, but I thought the point valid.

He hit me, and he hit me hard. A straight punch, no warning, right in the chin. It knocked me back, but I was amazed to find my body responding in kind: fists bunched up, ready to take a swing of my own. I over-ruled my base instincts, opting to step forward and knee him in the testicles instead, driving all of my weight up into that one point, until he crumpled with a satisfying groan.

He was suspended: our school had a no-closed-fists policy. If you ask me today, I think I'd still rather receive a punch to the face than a knee to the balls, but the policy made about as much sense as any other school rule, now that I look back.

No gum, because the people who bring gum to school in contravention of the rule tend to stick it underneath desks. No talking in class, because people don't communicate in the real world. No collaboration, for the same reason. Do your own work. Every child is an island, whether they work well that way or not.

My school years weren't bad, though. I discovered a love of honest fiction: fiction that didn't claim to be anything else, or did so in a novel or satirical framework. I made friends, good friends, and discovered that, while nobody around me shared my particular concerns and passions, they were building dreams and directions of their own.

There's an over-used quote from Marshall McLuhan, that everyone is doing the best they can with the resources they have. I grew to see that in my classmates. Unfortunately, it has a lesser-used corollary, that if your 'resources' consist of boundless greed and a lust for power, we end up with the shit-storm of a society that surrounds us now.

As I aged, I realised that the school system wasn't really worth fighting against. It was a contained microcosm of power, offering a haven to the odd petty tyrant, but ultimately a reflection and extension of more insidious societal ills.

That's what started me off, anyway, and I've been seeking appropriate responses ever since. It's hard, when you're one person facing something as broad as a sick and decaying culture, but hey, Batman managed, so I figure I've got a shot.

07 - CAPTURING THE MOMENT

How do you start out, once you've got a direction, and a long way to go? I think it was Confucius – so it was probably Lao-Tzu – who suggested "with a single step," but that was in the days before cars.

I've seen too many people fall to apathy in the face of monumental tasks, and I was pretty close myself. Photography was my first salvation.

Have you stared through the clean, unbiased glass of a lens? Have you pressed the shutter, and watched as the world is flattened into a simple two-dimensional image? Photography reveals a simplicity, a cleanliness that we don't get to experience otherwise. It takes something as simple as a shadow and elevates it to a statement; something as complex as a circuit-board and reduces it to a pattern.

I'm not talking about the instant gratification of the smart-phone camera, or the soulless plastic lenses that film the minutiae of people's lives: this is the essence of real photography, the difference between trying to hold on to a moment and trying to capture the best photograph of a moment. Photographer or participant: you can't be both.

A basic no-brand 2MP camera got me started, then I worked my way up to last-year's third-tier DSLR. Second-hand, of course, along with a pre-loved tripod and lenses.

I'm not a bad photographer. I've been offered a few wedding gigs, but I couldn't bring myself to support an institution so exploitative of couples looking to celebrate their love.

The money involved at every stage of Western wedding planning is nothing short of obscene.

Street photography was more my thing, and it provided an intimate, accessible way to chip away at the falsehoods that line and support our cultures, to visually expose the creeping lines of decay that they conceal.

From the moment I captured a discarded chocolate wrapper, the logo still visible through a coating of slime as it inched its way toward a storm-water drain, I was hooked. It may not sound like much, but photography modified my view of society: it was still an enormous dam beside my insect self, but each photo was a tiny hole, punched directly through those massive walls, letting the fetid water start to prickle out.

I hosted an exhibition, once, drawing inspiration from Banksy, an idol of mine. Rather than trying to approach a "legitimate" gallery, I printed some of my shots, then pinned them up in a train station. Security came and removed them after a few minutes, but I had backup copies.

One of my proudest memories is sliding the second set of crisp new prints from my folder, taking them one by one and pinning them in a precisely haphazard layout on a bare section of the wall.

Then Security came and removed me from the station. Not quite up to Banksy standards, but I retained my anonymity, and several passers-by did look interested.

Punch enough tiny holes, and the mess is hard to deny.

Where was I going with that? I tend to get distracted at times

- it's the problem with taking on the entire system at once, and the reason that bite-sized chunks are recommended.

Let me check back: Mild childhood trauma, disillusionment, fatalism... photography - how did that get in there?

Never mind. It's all relevant, more or less, and there's no time to fix it now. Let's just move on, shall we?

08 - BY ANY OTHER NAME

Photography may have helped give me a little perspective, a little hope, but I still needed a prompt to make me really come to terms with who and what I am.

That prompt was Odd Bob. Odd Bob was not his legal name, in case you're wondering, and I don't know if he was ever really a Robert.

Odd Bob was a thespian, a true method actor, and I met him as he performed an ongoing piece as a homeless man.

At first, I thought the poor, crooked figure *was* a homeless man. It was an easy mistake to make. His clothes reeked of unmentionable fluids, like piss and rotting feet, and his eyes were wild and bloodshot. A cloud of alcoholic vapour did little to mask the other scents, and he lurched toward me from an alleyway, forcing me to defensively reach into my pocket and fling a handful of change in his direction.

I'm one of the few individuals in London who still use cash on a regular basis. It's marginally harder to track, except by the process of elimination, and I refuse to let the banks profit from my meagre savings. Wages go into my bank account, only because that's hard to avoid these days, then I withdraw them.

The money doesn't go under my mattress, or into an easily-stolen safe: I keep it safely hidden in the bottom of a cereal box, stashed in the bathroom cabinet. I haven't had a mishap for at least two years, when a flatmate decided to throw out the misplaced cereal.

So that's why I had a handful of change in a decidedly plastic economy. And it struck Odd Bob square in the face.

Well, not so much "square" as in a spattering hail, but his face took the brunt of the deluge.

My instincts warred, I'm ashamed to say, for a fraction of a second: my defensive reflex became genuine sorrow, but I also wanted to whip out my camera and catch the damaged victim of society as he clutched his face and moaned on the ground. Instead, I clenched my nostrils and forced myself to help him up. I offered to buy him a cup of tea, and my journey to salvation was begun.

Odd Bob performed all over London. A one-man tour de force, his favourite character remained the homeless beggar.

"It's one of the few performances that can penetrate even those who disdain drama, m'boy," He told me, his voice strained like a real alcoholic's. "And my takings from *Home on the Street* are consistently higher than even the lofty heights of classical theatre."

Admittedly, Odd Bob didn't really have the voice for a rousing Shakespearean delivery, unless maybe he was playing the villainous Iago or a raving Hamlet – but nor did he have the patience for criticism.

"I'm not saying I'm better than Shakespeare," he intimated once, "But I think the money speaks for itself."

After Odd Bob described his lifestyle, I was intrigued. I may have little talent for drama, but alternative responses to this world were of obvious interest to me.

Odd Bob explained that he, too, was weary of farce and manipulation, and offered me the secret of true living for nothing more than the cup of tea.

Well, that and a small sum to compensate him for the time away from his performance.

And another, larger sum, so he could get his face checked out. I was embarrassed enough not to ask why he would need money when public health-care is free, but I suspected the obvious scam was a part of his character: Odd Bob made for an incredibly convincing homeless person.

So, what was his secret of true living? I'll get to that, but first there are some things you need to know, a primer, if you will.

09 - MIXING METAPHORS

"If wishes were horses, your mother's a whore!" There was laugher around the table, quickly muffled. That might have had something to do with my glare.

We were the only group in the pub, if you excluded a couple of old men who studiously ignored us as they sipped their pints and whispered about better days.

I took a deep breath and a quick sip of beer before responding. The glass was chill with condensation against my dry skin, and the lager flowed down easily, washing away my immediate frustration. Barnaby helped, too, his wet nose nudging my leg under the table, begging for a scratch. "That's not how the game works, Frank. You're meant to take two different proverbs or metaphors and combine them inappropriately. You've just taken one and turned it into a joke."

He smirked back at me, and was about to respond when Josh interrupted. "Oh, so you wanted something more like: No man is worth a thousand words?'"

"Thanks Josh. Frank certainly isn't, that's for sure. The game is about subverting language, undermining dominant power structures by re-appropriating figures for our own purposes, and training ourselves to actually *think* about the words. Another example would be 'You can lead a horse to water, but blood is thicker.'"

"Whoa, a little early in the evening for thinking, isn't it?" Frank palmed his face in mock pain. "Why are we playing this game again?" Barnaby chose that moment to let out a canine snort, which I pointedly ignored.

"We are playing this game because there is an enormous industry all around us, built on using language as a currency. Advertising companies are turning our words into their pawns, corrupting and undermining their very meanings, and this so-called game is a way to remind ourselves that the real meanings matter. There are people out there, right now, picking the next crop of words to turn to their own vile uses."

"Ah, the boogeymen are coming to get us."

"That's not it at all, Frank. Have you even read *1984*?"

"I wasn't even *born* in 1984. And I don't read."

I measured him across the table, trying to tell if he was serious. "You're joking. Everyone's read *1984*."

"Martin," his voice suddenly dropped an octave, crawling across the tabletop ominously as his finger beckoned me closer, ready to share a secret. Against my better judgement, I leaned in. "I'm dyslexic. I... I can't read."

How do you correct a faux pas of that magnitude? "I'm sorry, Frank, I had no idea." I felt a blush spreading over my face. "How did you get through school?"

His face darkened, and he leaned back. "Oh, sorry, did I say 'dyslexic?' I meant 'lazy'. Is that how this game works?"

Josh burst out laughing, while I clutched for my remaining pride, and sought an appropriate comeback. I settled for "You bastard." which slid off Frank's smug grin without leaving a ripple, and downing the remainder of my pint, which at least made me feel better.

"You'd have to talk to my parents about that, but I don't think it's a metaphor, or a proverb. Does that mean the newspeakers win?"

"So you do know *1984.*"

"Well who doesn't?"

I sighed, and irritation replaced the embarrassment. "Okay, if you're going to be a prick, how about 'Every dog has his drink, for tomorrow we die.'" Barnaby's head lifted at the mention of "dog," then slumped back down on my foot.

Frank's expression morphed into exaggerated confusion. "That's king prick to you, and I think I get it: does it mean the next round's on you?"

My friends are wonderful people, but can tend to be too obsessed with the immediate. At least *she* humours me, even if she doesn't share the depth of my passion, or always respect it.

She walked into the bar and automatically slapped Frank on the back of the head. "Hey guys, whatcha doing?"

"Ouch! Hiya Shel, we're drinking now - Martin tried to teach us some bullshit word game, but it's Friday night."

"Ignorance is a man's best friend, huh?" Frank choked on his beer, but we all laughed.

Her voice deepened, "You know they're out there right now? Unsleeping, unceasing, twisting our words until they are no longer ours at all?"

That's why I love her. Even if she was mocking me.

10 - THE FIXERS

Fred unlocked the office door with his thumbprint, automatically deactivating the alarm. The panel was cold beneath his skin, suggesting that the air-con was still temperamental. It was going to be another long day.

The night shift had collated and carefully stacked their papers, as expected, and the computer monitors were dark. The two desks sat waiting for Fred and his colleague, who trundled in sluggishly behind him.

With the aura of long practise, they sank simultaneously into their chairs, which let out leathery whispers under their weight.

Fred spoke first, trying to muster some pre-caffeinated enthusiasm. "Okay, Winston, what's on the chopping block today?"

"Literally."

"No, not literally, gobshite: what words are we reclaiming for the Organisation today?"

"No, I mean it's 'literally', Fred. We've got to come up with a strategy to corrupt the word 'literally'."

"Hmm, well, first of all, we don't say corrupt - we're not done realigning that word yet." Sometimes he thought his partner was deliberately winding him up. This was a by-the-book agency, and the last place you wanted to dick around with language.

He forced himself to let it go, and continued, "Realignment of 'literally', though, that might be easier than most. It's already woefully misused in online discussion. Have you read the top 5 release from MI5 this week?"

"Er, what's that?"

"Oh come on, Winston, are you still not checking your emails? MI5 release a list of their most amusing wiretaps each week; it's usually got some crackers on it.

"Hang on, let me pull the last one up. Here we go: 'I've just pinched off the biggest shit of my life. It took literally an hour to get out!'"

"I dunno, that doesn't sound like it would be near the top of their list. Teens write that sort of crap all of the time."

"Yeah, but this is a text-message from Tony Blair to his wife."

"Tony who?"

"Oh dear God, you don't get out, do you? Our former puppet minister for England? Never mind, it's not funny now, you've ruined it."

"Don't sulk, Fred, I'm sorry. I'm just a little slow on current events. That message wasn't misusing literally anyway, was it?"

"Oh, you need the context for that - he was only in the bathroom for five minutes, according to the GPS in his phone."

"Ah. So how does that help us to reclaim 'literally'?"

"Well, it doesn't, but it gives us an example of how it's already being realigned, without our help. Oh, shit."

"What is it?"

"I bet it isn't. Let me check." His hands were flying over the keyboard even before the monitor had flickered to life.

"There! Fucking admin! The reason 'literally' is being so beautifully and organically realigned is that they stuffed up the register again. Bloody Anubhav down in LA has been working on 'literally' for the past month."

"Is that a literal month, then?"

"Oh, very droll, Winston. Call Annie and get her to correct the register and send us some other word. I'm not going to re-tread wonder-boy's steps."

It was going to be a long day, indeed. Which happened to be the next word on Annie's list.

Fred opened a new document and began to type.

11 - MILE HIGH

Travelling these days is an unsettling experience. Flight is the only long-distance method that's financially viable to we lower classes of society, despite being the fastest option. The only highlight is that if you're inside the plane, you're sealed away from whatever chemicals they're dropping outside.

Since 9/11, the security theatre that surrounds air travel has also become the most distasteful.

A train is easy enough to derail, if you've got no conscience and a yearning for mindless terrorism. A ship can be damaged in any number of ways, and normal vehicular traffic is rife with opportunities for bloodshed. Why, then, is air travel the one area where we are expected to be subjected to invasive, chilling levels of scrutiny?

If you're following in my footsteps, trying to walk a more righteous path, your response to this ridiculous routine truly matters.

I don't remember what it was like beforehand, not really. I can't properly recall the freedom of checking in, having my bags x-rayed for obvious hijack-ready devices, then wandering happily into the boarding lounge.

Now it's jackets off, phones out, belts down, cross your eyes and hope you don't get chosen for a quick grope.

And that's if you're not transiting through the US. America frequently takes the obnoxious to an art-form, but the TSA are at the uncontested pinnacle of that trend.

Shoes off, trousers down, we know you're carrying something. Oh, our mistake, the wand wasn't configured properly. Next stop, pat down, oops sir, what big balls you have! You don't mind a little squeeze, do you, not in the name of keeping everyone else feeling safe and warm?

The boarding lounge has become a space to recover, to rock back and forth while you brush down the anger and frustration of being treated with less respect and human decency than a convicted criminal. I'll give you a word of advice for free: don't smile. Nobody could possibly be enjoying the process, so your cheery grin is immediately suspicious.

I should amend that: don't smile, unless you want to be taken aside for a special level of intimacy with the screeners. Trust me, you don't.

When the real threat is the government, any pantomime of security is just that, a farce, a puppet show. I believe it's our responsibility to demonstrate this at every opportunity, but I also don't want to miss my flight. This can be a difficult balance to strike, but I think I'm getting the hang of it.

"Why?"

"Excuse me, sir?"

"I said, why? Why do I have to remove any liquids from my bag?"

"Sir, it's our security policy. If you could just comply, as quickly as possible."

"But what threats can my liquids possibly contain?"

"'I'm not at liberty to discuss that, sir, but please be assured that it's for your own safety."

"Well, I don't have any liquids in my bag."

"Okay, sir, can you please empty your pockets and walk over here."

"What is it?"

"It's a metal detector."

"No, it appears to be a back-scatter x-ray machine."

"Why did you ask then, if you knew what it was?"

"Because I wanted to see if you would be honest with me."

"I'm just the screener, sir, I couldn't care less what the machine is called. It beeps if you're concealing anything on your person, that's all I know - it's a metal detector to me."

"It beeps, as you put it, because an agent sitting in a room somewhere is shown an image of my naked body and my clothing when I stand there. He or she then presses the alert button to indicate a possible issue if they see anything they consider suspicious."

"Glad to hear it, sir. Can you please just step into the machine?"

"Only if you can tell me when it was last calibrated."

"I tested it this morning myself."

"Not tested. Calibrated. To ensure the radiation level is correct."

"Sir, please stop talking about radiation. You'll disturb the other passengers."

"They should be disturbed. Did you know that many of these machines are improperly calibrated, and that an incorrect setting can send harmful levels of radiation onto passengers' skin?"

"Sir, if you'll just lower your voice, and step into the machine."

"No, I don't believe I will."

"Okay, sir, then you can choose to have a pat-down instead."

"That's hardly a choice, is it? I can be violated visually, and potentially exposed to harmful levels of radiation, or I can select a tactile violation, where I'm groped by a stranger."

"I'm feeling less like a stranger every second, sir. In fact, I feel like I know you quite well."

"Do I have a third option, at all? Could I perhaps sign a statement that I'm not carrying any explosive devices?"

"Sir, did you just use the word 'explosive'? I'm afraid I'll need you to step this way."

"And this is supposed to be the land of the free? I can't even say explosive in the correct context?"

"You said it again! Joe, a hand? We've got a threat over here."

"No, that's not what I meant - come on, you were asking me."

"Sorry sir, policy is policy, and you're going to have to explain yourself to security. Leave your shoes here."

So I might need a little more practice, but at least I'm learning where schools get their zero-tolerance stupidity from.

I realise that flight is itself a perfect opportunity for multiple governments to update their data on us, but am also aware that it's one of the concessions we most often have to make: we can't always avoid travel, but we can ensure we scrutinise the system and hold it to account while we're at it.

12 - STRANGE ATTRACTION

Trust isn't easy when the system is out to get you - to get everyone, by design - but Shelley had opened up a tiny gap in my armour. Odd Bob managed to slip through on our first encounter, but even so I felt awkward meeting new people.

A common piece of advice is to be yourself, to be open and honest when making a first impression (and ideally thereafter). Whoever gave that advice has clearly never dated my girlfriend.

Before meeting her friends for the first time, I was terrified. Of Shelley, that is. She stopped me outside the pub and went over it again.

"Okay, Martin, I'll ask again: please be on your best behaviour." She didn't quite waggle her finger at me, but it was there in spirit.

"I appreciate the vote of confidence, Shel, but they're just your friends. Don't you want them to see the real me?"

"It might be a little early in the relationship for that, Martin - just give them the watered-down version we've discussed."

"It still feels like you want me to change for you."

"That feeling is accurate - well done."

"I know you love the real me, Shel, and this is who I am. I can't just turn myself on and off."

"No, but I can certainly turn you on - or off. Your choice."

"Fine, fine, I'll avoid those topics. What was the list again?"

"Religion, politics, music, capitalism, air-travel, systems of governance, history, sports and film. I think that's about it."

"You just snuck film in there. What can I possibly say about that to upset people?"

"It's not what you'd say to upset people, it's what you'd say to embarrass me. Were you, or were you not the one parroting that idiocy about *The Shining* as Kubrick's confession to faking the moon landing?"

"I wouldn't call it idiocy..."

"The prosecution rests."

"Fine. I solemnly swear to be good."

"Okay, let's head in."

The bar was to become our regular spot. Tucked away from the street, its unassuming face hid a surprising range of beverages, and less-surprising but passable food. An older couple ran it, and seemed more interested in letting an authentic air of disrepair develop than seeking new business. The seats were intact, mostly, and the booths had that level of comfort only attainable through years of heavy arses pounding them into submission. The tables were equally worn, and the lighting dim, but it was cleanish, and our table was always free. That came later, of course.

"Frank, Josh, Zara. This is Martin, he'll be forgetting your names presently."

A man stood up. He was big: not fat, but large, substantial. Built, I think they'd call it. With his dark skin and short, perfectly-sculpted hair, he could have been a model for products of equal substance - cologne, or some other toiletry requiring manly endorsement. He smiled, then, and transformed into a young boy, ready to yank the legs from a toad and slip the twitching body down your back.

Not that I would condone animal cruelty of any kind, or find it amusing, for the record.

He extended a hand, and for the first time in my life, I honestly searched for a joy-buzzer before taking it. "Good to finally meet the elusive man in Shel's life. I'm Frank, in case her dignified introduction didn't make it clear, hope she isn't riding you too hard."

"Frank!" That was the first time I had seen Shelley blush. I liked it.

"Gah, you've got a filthy mind, Shelley, not like that." He swivelled his head and winked lewdly at me, then continued the rotation, presenting Shelley with a perfectly innocent expression. His face was like rubber, and he knew it: seeing my amazed stare, he deliberately nodded his head while waggling an ear, maintaining a perfect poker face all the while.

"Aw, stop showing off, Frank. Martin will be sick of your shit soon enough."

Shelley nodded past his head at the speaker. "Zara, play nice."

Zara was beautiful. That's not accurate. Zara was Beautiful. Hair down to her... Eyes like... A face... She was indescribable, really, beyond comparison. Until she opened her mouth. The illusion shattered, piece by piece, as she began to speak.

"Shelley does this thing, where she'll over-prepare for anything. I'm not saying that in a mean way, I mean, she's adorable, and I love her to bits, but you don't want to let her make any plans."

She hardly paused for breath, which led to a pleasing moment of distraction as her lungs inflated, then continued, "There was this one time, and I'd missed my bus that morning, but Josh came and picked me up. He's got a really nice car, and he's such a sweetie. Where was I? Oh, yeah, so Shelley was planning our weekend away, and when we arrive she pulls out this list of banned topics."

She had an incredibly normal voice, and it washed over her, transforming wind-swept savannahs, lush with life and promise, into hair. Just hair; pretty enough, but nothing otherworldly about it. Red, with a slight wave, it curled around an admittedly shapely face, framing a pretty upturned nose and lips the colour of over-ripe watermelon flesh, parted as though about to breathe a dark, dirty secret.

I had never really understood the term cognitive dissonance until each utterance from that moist opening crashed into me in all its mundanity, breaking her spell anew.

I became suddenly aware of Shelley, watching me watching Zara. I closed my mouth, wondering how long it had lain open. Zara continued speaking, which helped. A lot.

The tangents were flying thick and fast, and my libido retreated under the assault. She was still going.

"She's got it all typed up and everything, but she writes it on the fridge, says it's so we can see it. Only she uses a permanent marker, and we had to find some spirits to remove it before we left, and the only thing we could use was vodka, but it was a really pricey bottle."

She sounded like a stereotypical bubblegum-chewing waitress from some American diner. On speed. Less the accent.

Josh interjected then, a quieter, less dominant figure. His voice was soft, pleasant, and I liked him immediately, partly because of the distraction, "Shel's a one-woman censor, all right, but her heart's in the right place, eh guys?" I mentally compared the two versions, blinked, and decided Josh was my preferred story-teller.

Frank downed his drink, then replied, "Good point, Josh - bet you a tenner she's done the same thing to Martin. So spill, new guy, what's on the list?"

"Oh... There was no list. Shel trusts me." A stretch. I felt my own face start to twitch at the deception, but they had already moved on in a whirlwind of curiosity.

"Yeah, right. Shel, spill. What are Martin's taboo topics?"

"I don't think you want to open this can of worms, Frank."

"Oh, but I do. The best conversations are the ones you don't want us to have. Please?"

"Don't blame me, then. Martin, why don't you tell them how you feel about dancing? Josh and Frank both do Ceroc, and Zara is a Grade Six tap-dancer."

"Dance? Come on, Shel, that's weak, even for you. Give us the good stuff. Martin, what's your favourite topic? What are you the most passionate about?"

There was only one correct answer to that: "You mean aside from Shelley?"

"Oh, very smooth, the man's been practising. But yeah, aside from Shelley. If I asked you what the most critical, important thing in the world today is, aside from love - to keep our lunches down - what would you say?"

"Hmm. It's not a straightforward question, but I suppose if I had to summarise my concerns about the world, I'd have to say I'm worried about a lack of transparency and trust at all levels from the government up."

"You mean the government down?"

"Not really: I'm talking about our espoused model of society, where the government is at the bottom level of the hierarchy, serving the will and the needs of the people, with the corporate whoremongers at the opposite end."

"Whoremongers - I like that!" Frank interrupted, but I ignored him and continued.

"In reality, of course, those corporations act as a counter-weight, with them and the government rotating around the pivot-point of consumerism, and us left dizzy in the middle. We have no choice but to be suspicious, to treat them as malicious entities doing their best to keep us off balance and at their mercy."

"I like him, Shelley, you can keep him." Zara and Josh rolled their eyes simultaneously as Frank spoke. I kept my own on Josh, it was safer that way.

"Wait until you have to play one of his games." Shelley joked. I hoped she was joking.

"Shouldn't you keep those in the bedroom?"

"Not those games, and wouldn't you like to know?"

I decided to change the topic, although I'm sure they had already spotted my crimson cheeks. "So, Josh, what do you do with yourself?"

"Nice segue, Martin. I'm an architect..."

Zara interrupted immediately, "And if you believe that, then we rescind Shelley's permission to date you. He does have a nice car - I think I mentioned that earlier, but he's only a junior assistant at an architecture firm."

"That must be interesting?"

"That's one word for it. I'd like to say I do most of the real work..."

"And he will if you let him..." Frank speaking now. The group really had their patter down. I briefly wondered how many guys Shelley had introduced to them, then decided I didn't want to know.

"... Please, I was going to say: but I mainly keep the office running smoothly - ferry files around, order stationery, that kind of thing. I'm studying architecture part-time, so I'll be on the team before long." Josh looked hopeful.

"... If his firm accepts an online diploma."

"It's accredited, toss-pot. Speaking of, why don't you tell Martin what you do, Frank, in case Shelley hasn't warned him?"

"I don't know if he's ready to withstand my awesomeness, that's all."

"That won't be a problem, he's dating Shel, remember?"

"Okay, I'll play. My name is Frank, and I'm an alcoholic. A damn good one, too, but that's my superhero identity. By day, I provide a comprehensive range of custodial services to several large multi-national clients."

"You're a janitor, Frank."

"For large multi-national clients, Zara."

"Ignore him, Martin - he's there by choice, but he likes to pretend he's an oppressed minority." Zara replied. Shelley glanced a warning across before I could offer my input on oppressed minorities.

"In case you're even slower than Shelley suggested," She winked at Shel, and I caught my breath again, unsuccessfully willing my mind not to go where it already was. "I'm Zara, and I'm a fully qualified teacher."

"A school teacher?"

"That is the general usage of the word, yes. I'm trained to high-school level, although I'm interested in many areas, and thought of becoming a maths teacher, or maybe a biologist - that was after I decided against the police force -

but I'm currently with junior students, 7-8 year-olds."

"Careful, Zara, whatever you do, don't get Martin started on education."

"I'm sure he's not that bad, are you, Martin?" She batted her eyelashes at me. She had incredibly expressive eyelashes. Shelley was still staring at me.

"Er, I try," I stammered "but education is a fascinating topic."

Shelley interrupted before I could make my statement any more inane, and directed the conversation to safer waters. We discussed dance after all, and Frank kept us in turns entertained and disgusted for the rest of the afternoon.

Shelley debriefed me afterward, walking home from the pub.

"You did well, Martin, much better than I expected."

"I did? I mean, of course I did."

"It's okay, I know what they're like. Josh is lovely, but you can trust the other two about as far as you can swing a cat."

I grinned at her mixed metaphor, then felt a little sick for the hypothetical cat.

"Oh, and don't think I didn't see you checking out Zara."

"I... Bu... Er..."

"Oh, it's fine, Martin. I'm not some fumbling teenager, and people aren't possessions. You've got eyes, haven't you? The girl is gorgeous."

"That's an understatement." I mumbled, under my breath.

"But she's got no filter. There's no bigger turn-off than verbal diarrhoea, and that girl has it in spades."

"So I take it you won't be leaving me for Zara?" I managed, once my brain caught up with me. Why do straight men seem hardwired to find lesbian fantasies the pinnacle of distraction?

"Not so long as you don't leave me for Josh."

"Josh? So he isn't with Zara?"

"Not likely. They're best friends, but Josh is a gay as a... gay person."

"That was a pretty limp-wristed comparison for you."

"Yeah, but I've seen what he's gone through with his family. We all did, and Josh is bloody lucky to be here today. I don't joke about sexuality, not since then."

"They didn't take it well?"

"That's an understatement. His mother went full religious nut-job, wanted to 'cure him'. If it had been the 60s, I'm sure she would have had him committed."

"Ouch, poor bastard."

"Yeah, although I think he'd prefer to be a bastard, or adopted. His dad was better, but only by comparison.

Here's a cultural dynamic for you, should tie nicely into your theories: if people keep on perpetuating stereotypes about gay individuals, then it enables people like his mother, even in these relatively enlightened times. Hell, you've probably heard people using the type of lines I mean. 'She's bi, it means she can't make up her mind,' or, worse, 'she's bi, it means she's promiscuous.'"

"I think I've heard a variant on the second one…"

"I know, I was moderating my language. But that, Martin dearest, is why you won't hear me making light of who people are. Not when it comes to the building blocks of their identity, anyway. I'll still be making fun of Frank's pretension."

"Glad to hear it."

"And your conspiracies."

"Not so glad to hear it."

"We'll be fine, dear, now give me a kiss and tell me where you're taking me tonight. You survived the first hurdle, and I feel like a celebration."

Having people to confide in, a place to really belong, it was a new experience. Some clichés are clichés for a reason, and friendship really did make it easier for me to value my cause. It's one thing to fight for a principle or an ideal. It's quite another to struggle on behalf of people you love, even if they don't quite recognise the cause.

I had friends before I met Shelley, of course. That is, I had co-workers, acquaintances, even a drinking buddy or two.

But London is a city of transients, and I had no permanent friendships, no sense of home until her and the gang accepted me.

Between them and Odd Bob, my guard was lower than ever before.

13 - I SPY

I can recall every mumble of my first apologetic conversation with Odd Bob, but it's what followed that truly cemented our friendship.

The secret of truth isn't something you're offered every day. I'm assuming, there, but I think it's a safe one. I couldn't pass up such a chance, so I followed him as he led me on a crooked path through the city. There's a trick to navigating in London, but I never learned it. One cobblestone-shod street looks much like another, and the old stone buildings bleed into a murky colour carousel in your short-term memory.

In short, I was soon lost. To top it off, the twists and turns were making my dizzy, so I stopped Odd Bob and asked him about the strange route. That's when he taught me the first tenet of a lower-risk life outside the system: avoiding CCTV cameras.

"They're almost everywhere, m'boy, little glass eyes, unblinking and vigilant! Almost, that is. Ol' Odd Bob, he knows the ways, he walks in the cracks." He'd sometimes do that, slip into the third person and swing between vague riddles and lucid explanations, but I was already getting used to his performance.

"It's an invisible statement against the surveillance state, an ironic means of protest. An' it keeps me from the coppers' grasp. Don' want be arrested for panhandling, would have to break character to explain m'self to the law."

In fact, Odd Bob never really broke character, which was inspiring, and contributed to my growing admiration. I trailed in his wake, reassured by his explanation and glad that

I wasn't downwind, until we eventually arrived at a plain-looking building on a plain-looking street. He ducked down a set of stairs, and through a door-less doorway into a gloomy basement.

Basements are almost always gloomy, but this one was helped along by a generous coating of mold and grime. Even the floor was sticky, making odd little sucking noises beneath my sneakers. Boxes were stacked, to use a generous description, around the room, which extended off into deeper darkness. A handful of lights flickered at uneven intervals, and I soon realised the flickering was because they were oil lamps, burning something rancid, if the smell was any indication.

Odd Bob limped towards one particular collection of boxes, and for the first time, I doubted him.

What was I doing, following some strange character into a dark and filthy basement?

It was the sort of place mothers wouldn't even need to warn their children about: the natural habitat of leering clowns bearing cleavers, of card-carrying child-carrying creeps and the truly disturbed. There was no room for the clean or the bright, and the very sunlight itself quailed in the face of that oppressive room.

My doubt soon turned to shame, as Odd Bob knocked politely on a grease-stained box, and an old woman appeared. Not magically, of course - she actually took some time to push the flap of her box open and clamber out - but the result was the same.

She had wrinkles on her wrinkles, and dirt on top of those. I couldn't tell if she was Romany or some other ethnicity - it was hard to discern skin tone in the murky light, and I already had a fundamental dislike of stereotypes and arbitrary categorisation. She did look wise, and when she spoke she confirmed some origin exotic to me, at least, although probably less so to her own people.

Odd Bob whispered in her ear for a few moments, then the woman turned to me and smiled. I wished immediately that she hadn't: dental hygiene was obviously not a priority in that basement. She continued the grin, and I did my best not to back away, look scared, or to inhale. I managed one out of three, and my pride allowed me to keep from shaking at the addition to Odd Bob's aroma.

"Our mutual friend hass told me zhat you seek truce?"

"Truce?"

"No, truuuuce. You desire za truce of ze vorld around you, da?" Her patois was an impressive combination of every awfully-portrayed gypsy mystic, and I reacted instinctively, with a whisper.

"Y..yes. Odd Bob told me that you have some sort of truth to offer?"

"Odd Bob - " She glanced oddly - how else? - at him, then continued "speaks za truce. I haf an inner I." I took only a second to translate the second "I" to "eye," and mentally congratulated myself.

"So you can see the future?"

"Da, I see so many futures, so many thinks... But for you, I see only one pass."

"One pass? Oh, one path?"

"Da, one pass. You shall walk zis pass blindfolded. I can show you your pass, but you must first complete ze ancient rite."

"I'm, I'm sorry, I don't know the ancient rite."

"No matter. I shall guide you. It is symbol only, but you must cross my palm with silver."

By this stage, I had discovered a newfound respect for Hollywood's portrayal of seers. I had, to my shame, suspected a heavy fictional bias in the decrepit crones crouched leering over their crystals balls in so many cheesy epics, but this encounter had swiftly confirmed the converse: our conversation could have slid seamlessly from the screen. I withdrew a coin from my pocket, squinting to check the colour in the darkness.

"Will this work?"

She peered down at my hand, and scowled. "Do not offend ze spirits, boy. Ze silver is a token of value, of worth." Odd Bob leapt to the rescue.

"Martin, m'boy, how much money do you have with you?"

I checked my wallet. "Hard to tell in this light, but about fifty pounds."

Odd Bob looked disappointed, and started to shake his head. My heart sank. The seer watched us for a moment, and then spoke.

"I haf consulted ze spirits, and zey will accept your offering, zis time." Her aged claw darted out and snatched the cash from my hand. She counted the crumpled notes and made them vanish, flickering into nowhere before my eyes. Then she smiled that terrifying smile again, while I surreptitiously wiped my hand on my jeans.

"You are a lucky boy, Martin, few get to negotiate with the spirits. Now listen closely, and listen well. What must be said can be said only once, for your ears only."

I leaned forward, immune to the stench in the face of this rare encounter. When she spoke again, it was in a croak.

"You haf come far, young Martin. You haf come far indeed, but your pass ahead is short." I gulped, not liking the prediction so far, but she glared me into silence before I could speak.

"Short, but not in time." I relaxed, although I didn't understand her words.

"Ze spirits haf watched over you, haf kept you safe, and will do so in the future. Zey tell you," she started to shake, "zat everysing is connected... Zat you should seek ze pattern."

She shuddered, and her breath came faster. "Ze pattern will make everysing clear, but you haff to, haf to..." She paused, then stared deep into the darkness... "Haf to beware ze all-seeing eyes." She slumped, done, and let out a sighed entreaty: "Now go, Martin, Odd Bob will see you out."

14 - A QUEST!

I never did find out her name, Odd Bob's foreboding friend, but I spent weeks looking for the pattern.

Her prophecy seems a little vague when I examine it now, but you really had to be there. It sounded so much deeper when she said it.

Everything was connected. If that was true, then my meeting Odd Bob was fated.

I visited him every day or two on his corner, and we walked, sipped tea from a faded thermos, avoided the CCTV cameras, and discussed possible components of the pattern.

It wasn't hard to figure out, not really. There was no holy grail to battle for, just an enormous jigsaw to assemble from the millions of pieces floating around us.

Odd Bob and I pooled our existing pieces, and soon discovered that we had a lot in common.

I taught him about the dangers of language regulation, and he opened my eyes to the secret chain around our collective necks, a chain forged in secrecy and subterfuge, and into which we willingly slipped our heads.

"They are all around us, m'boy. The glass eyes see, they hold us in thrall to the operatives who sit behind them. You buy a newspaper, a box is ticked. You hear a song, a box is ticked. A box is ticked... A box is ticked. A million mopper-uppers ticking bloody boxes in a maelstrom of clandestine consumerist claptrap." Odd Bob loved his alliteration.

I once took Barnaby with me to visit Odd Bob, but he got a little too excited by the smell. I think he meant to lick the fragrant trousers, that the bite was an accident, but I didn't want to risk a repeat performance.

Sometimes, we would leave Odd Bob's corner and make our crooked way to a pub. Outside a pub, really, as few proprietors would welcome Odd Bob and his distracting persona to the taproom. If it suited both our desire for secrecy and the sensibilities of the other patrons, it didn't bother us, but the alcohol never seemed to impart any new insights.

Still, over time, Odd Bob heightened my awareness of the "foot-soldiers of the network", as he called them. He challenged my perspective, forcing me to confront the forces arrayed against us as an ubiquitous mesh, with operatives acting at all levels, instead of the outdated hierarchy I'd been imagining.

The problem with this approach was that it multiplied my puzzle to new levels of complexity. Just when I thought I had connected Big Parking with Big Oil and Big Tobacco, Odd Bob's revelation sent me scrambling for another million pieces to fit between them.

Meanwhile, I was grappling with the question of whether fate had to be pursued, or could in actuality even be pursed. Self-fulfilling prophecy is an amusing and ironic mechanism in the world of fiction, but poses a problem when we're faced with a prophet in the real world. Do we respond consciously to their words, alter our actions accordingly, or try to go about our lives as we did before. Of course their prediction is going to have an impact, so was that itself fated?

If it's a true prophecy, the approach we choose is destined, by definition.

The seer had said that my path was singular, anyway, so I decided that the path of least resistance would be the nicest path for destiny to offer me. I could spend every waking hour trying to discern the pattern, or I could simply live my life, and let it resolve itself where and when it would.

15 - MORE THAN MEETS THE EYE

My endless discussions with Odd Bob contributed to a growing sense of urgency about my convictions. As each theory became more solid, more fully realised, it felt more immediate, and I became slightly frustrated with people who weren't concerned. Unfortunately, *people* included Shelley.

"I don't get you, Shel. I mean, you've read the same things I have, watched the same videos, and I've passed on the greater portion of Odd Bob's wisdom, yet you don't believe."

"I do believe, it's just my worldview has a slightly different emphasis: one less coloured by ignorance."

"Why do you always have to get me down?"

"Oh don't be a wuss. I love you, you know that, but your insistence on some ideas is just ridiculous, and your emphasis worse. I mean, you've worked in offices, yes?"

"Yeah, you know that."

"I do, but I'm making a point, dear, don't get smart. How would you respond to the quotation that people are promoted to their level of incompetence?"

"Anyone who's worked anywhere can tell you that. It's call the *Peter Principle*, I think, a common side-effect of merit-based work environments, where growth and promotion are required."

"Okay, then, I'm glad you're in agreement. Given that, why

would you attribute to conspiracy and manipulation what can be ascribed to incompetence?”

“I wouldn’t - I think there is plenty of room for both. There are dozens of cases - proven cases - where downright evil has been allowed and encouraged, because it happened to be the convenient solution.”

“And I’ll let you quote me chapter and verse on those later on, but for now we’re examining the crux of your belief: that some shadowy coalition of composers are writing the world’s biggest evil orchestra, and we’re all pre-ordering tickets by participating in their schemes.”

“I wouldn’t put it quite like that...”

“Yes you would. I’m quoting you, from last week. The analogy was too ridiculous to forget.”

“Oh.”

“Let me continue: given the way the modern workplace works, or doesn’t, isn’t it more likely that organisations are generally incompetent, that incompetence is in fact the default setting of most any human structure?”

She paused, while I wondered whether the question was rhetorical, then swept on.

“And if we extrapolate the incompetence we see every day in corporate London, a pattern emerges that could be viewed, in a certain light, as orchestrated evil, but that is more honestly recognised as an array of human cock-ups.”

“How does that explain the cover-ups, the scandals, then?”

"Flawlessly. In the first instance, we have the dominant inclination of an individual human facing the wrath of the faceless organisation that puts bread on their table: to cover their own arse. That's rule one from day one of our working lives. We learn how to justify, to explain, to shift blame, to urge conciliation and negotiation. Hell, conflict resolution is one of our most prized skills, and it's really about de-emphasising our errors.

"Humans fuck up. That's what we tell kids, if in slightly warmer language. Everyone makes mistakes. Honesty is the best policy.

"Can you imagine an office manager reporting to the executive team with those principles behind her? 'I know our profits are down 20%, but shit happens. Oh, and I may have clipped the CEO's car in the parking lot this morning.'"

She took a quick breath, then continued. "Secondly, incompetence is the only valid explanation for the cover-ups and scandals. A proper conspiracy would have severe consequences for the exposure of a scandal. If you're prepared to manipulate the entire supposedly free world, you're also going to euphemistically erase any minion who bucks the plan.

"Whistleblowers simply aren't an option if you posit a logical conspiracy. Even a basic threat analysis would highlight them as a major obstacle. Incompetence itself would be anathema to successful plans of the magnitude you're suggesting, as it would make everything contingent on an entire chain of weak links.

"Which all goes to suggest that even your criminal genius, after doing a primary-school brainstorm, would realise how the whole mess is likely to end up, and decide on something more viable to achieve their ends.

"Okay, okay, I get your point. But why can't both be true? Incompetence goes a long way toward explaining some things, but so do my theories, and there's a lot there that incompetence can't cover."

"Like what?"

"UFOs."

"Say what now?" She actually backed away from me, as though my mouth were foaming.

"You should see the look on your face. It was a joke, Shel, you need to step back and lighten up. You're over-simplifying the problem, positing a homogenous group of identical drones behind the schemes, and that assumption makes your argument hard to refute. I did see an interesting documentary the other week, though, suggesting that the Nazis escaped to a secret moon base."

"*Iron Sky* wasn't a documentary, Martin, do we have to have that talk?"

"Very funny - this was an actual scientist, positing that..."

"Oh, an actual scientist? Would that be one of the actual, grant-accepting, big-oil-corrupted, government-monitored scientists you've told me so much about? One of the architects of the largest intellectual lie in history, as a dear friend of mine put it just yesterday?"

"I'm buying dinner again, aren't I?"

"No, you're cooking. And I want something special, after this conversation. I might have been simplifying – to an extent – but that's better than making shit up, which is all you and your homeless friend seem to do sometimes."

"He's not –"

"Martin?"

"Yes dear?"

"Shut up."

16 - A PERFECT PLAN

The table was surrounded by identical old men in immaculate tailored suits. The Chair stood and ushered in their guest.

"Welcome everyone. I'd like to introduce Dr. Xu. She'll be presenting some intriguing research to assist with our long-term strategic planning."

"Thank you, sir. My colleagues and I are established authorities in the field of social micro engineering. You have probably come across our earlier work, in practise if not in our publications: we demonstrated how passive surveillance techniques could maintain the positive impact of micro-management, while avoiding the stigma of human micro-managers. This particular technique is now in use around the world, to great effect, and was based on the discovery that the knowledge someone was being watched was every bit as effective as a supervisor standing behind them, monitoring their work - but without the negative impact on their typing and other basic skills.

"This current research is a little more nuanced, but has major implications for projects such as your own."

"We have been tracking people's expectations with respect to workplace performance, and discovered a disturbing trend in the Organisation's holdings. In each of your businesses, productivity was simply too high, and failure rates far too low to be believed.

"You may rightly stop me now and exclaim that this doesn't sound like a bad thing, but I'm glad none of you have. To external observers, a superficial view of the statistics is more than enough to demonstrate that your companies are outliers on every performance metric we have.

"What you're forgetting, esteemed colleagues –" the men shuffled uncomfortably at the word, but she continued, oblivious "– is that people intuitively dislike the different. They have been trained to expect the odd

aggressive salesperson, the idiot guide, the trainee operator. People distrust utopias - you know this, it's why you sell them gritty 'realism'. People want apologies, scandals and, ultimately, humanity. They have issues in their own lives, they are all too aware that they're not perfect, and they don't want your companies to be any different.

"What we're suggesting is that we need to introduce some level of flexibility into staff and policy performance. Call it ineptitude, call it stupidity, but we need it, gentlemen, or your entire operation will be at risk."

"I'm not doubting your expertise, Miss –"His expression said otherwise.

"– Doctor." Hers remained impassive.

"I'm not doubting your expertise, Miss Doctor, but how exactly will our operation be at risk?"

"When the dominoes start to fall, sir, everyone will be in the spotlight. If yours are the only ones still standing, aren't even wobbling the slightest bit, who do you think the people will blame? People may be foolish, as a rule, but even they can manage basic arithmetic."

There was a brief silence as the men digested this concept, and contemplated the words. A few contemplated the Doctor's physical attributes, too, and wondered what the word of a woman was worth.

"So you're saying we destroy ourselves, too?" His conclusion was not singular, and his tone made it clear what he and his thought of silly little girls with silly little ideas.

"Not at all, sirs. I merely suggest you inject enough variance into your company skill-sets to let you appear to fall with the rest. A buffer, might be a good term for it; you could call it keeping up appearances. Or keeping them down, more accurately."

The Chair stood once more, and his tone lacked the contempt of the relatively junior member. "Thank you, Dr. Xu. Do you have any recommendation s on the practical steps we might take to implement such an approach?"

The others sighed inwardly. This was no democracy; it looked like they were going to dance to this frivolous tune. All paid more attention to the woman's next words.

"I do, sir, and they are outlined in-depth in this document. In summary, though, it's simple: fire your human resources department, or get them to stop examining the job applicants so thoroughly. Let a few less-capable workers move up the ranks, remove a few promising junior staff members - it all helps, and you'll be looking like normal, wholesome businesses in no time."

17 - ETHICAL CONVERSATIONS

Zara was the first to console me, after I was again restructured.

"How are you doing, Martin?"

"I'm getting there, Zara. It's a hard city to live in, sometimes."

"Yeah, I heard about the redundancy."

"It wasn't a redundancy. I was fired."

"Oh. That sucks."

"Yeah, it really does. But you could buy me a pot of tea, if you want to help?"

"I think I can almost splash out for that, on my salary."

"Rub it in, why don't you."

"Don't mind if I do. You'll find something else, anyway. Speaking of finding things, you didn't comment on my shoes. Hasn't Shelley taught you anything?"

So 'console' might have been a stretch, but it was good to think about something else. "They look nice. Are they new?"

"Psh. You don't ask that question, poor boy: you always assume a lady's shoes are new. And her clothes, for that matter."

"Your clothes are new, too?"

"No, I'm not made of money. But it makes a good impression

to act as though they are. I couldn't afford a new outfit this week – the shoes cost me hundreds."

"And probably pennies to make."

"I'd better tell Shelley to add clothing to her list of taboo topics. These are designer heels."

"I'm not the best person to talk to about fashion brands, Zara. I could tell you things about your shoes that would make you sick."

"Go on then, but I'll be throwing up on you."

"Did you know that most of the world's high-end brands are owned by a handful of parent corporations? They use multiple subsidiaries, and even compete against themselves. It's the ultimate global monopoly."

"Yes, as a matter of fact, I did know that. I've seen that infographic everyone keeps forwarding around. It was a few years out of date when I saw it, but I guess the facts haven't changed much..."

I jumped in quickly when she paused. "Well did you know that their holdings include stakes in many fashion and clothing labels?"

"Well duh! That was kinda the point, that they owned everything. I'm not tasting the bile yet. Why don't you tell me how you'd go about buying a pair of shoes?"

"If you wanted to make the purchase as ethically as possible, you'd firstly find a company who weren't publicly listed on the stock market, and privately-owned. Then you'd want to look at their supply chains. They should make their goods on site, using locally-sourced materials, from free-range, humanely raised and killed cattle. Finally, you would make sure the staff at each stage, including the show-room, are fairly treated and paid."

"Lesson for the day, Martin: don't ever underestimate a woman. If you underestimate Shelley, she'll be wearing your balls as a hideous but ethical pair of earrings. Not that she's ever done that, but I suspect she has it in her."

So you actually did your homework?

"Don't sound so surprised: I'm a teacher. Homework is one thing I have down. Aw, crap, keep your head really still."

"What is it? A wasp?"

"Worse, it's Sandy."

"Who or what is Sandy?"

"She's a really difficult acquai... A very good friend of mine - Martin, meet Sandy."

Sandy looked small and timid, but her words dispelled that immediate impression even as it formed. "Hola Zara, are you two bumpin' the ol' nasty?"

How do you respond to such a crass question, while you're still trying to chase the fantasy it creates from your mind? And other places. "Uh..."

"Sandy! That's no way to talk to a gentleman. Martin is Shelley's boy."

"What's he doing schmoozing with you, then, you sexy bitch? Nice Pradas, by the way, *tres chic.*"

That one word snapped me back to more familiar, comfortable territory. "Prada, huh?"

Zara blushed, but Sandy continued as though she hadn't noticed. "It's a fashion brand, Martin, I wouldn't expect a guy to know that. Those adorable shoes Zara's wearing are from their latest line." She ran her eyes over me, like she was examining a cut of steak. I suspected she took hers bloody.

"So, how'd you meet Shelley? Let me guess, she was selling herself down in King's Cross again, and you took her for the week, the little tramp?"

Zara came to my rescue. Sort of. "Do you have to be so fucking awful all the time, Sandy? They met online, like there's this game where you can pretend to be a wizard, a warrior, or a ..." She looked at me for help, and I automatically replied.

"... dozen other classes." She didn't look illuminated, but that didn't hinder her story.

"Whatever, that's not the point: the two of them sat up for hours talking, then met up and hit it off. Martin was a bit funny about meeting Shelley, but it turns out he's a conspiracy nut - no offense, Martin - so that's why he had all these strange conditions."

"Sounds too romantic for my tastes. What's wrong with a quick shag?"

I heard Frank's voice in my head, urging me on before I could stop myself. "The herpes, generally."

Zara burst out laughing, and clapped her hands. "There you go, Sands, a taste of your own medicine. "

I stammered to apologise, "Er, perhaps you'd care to join us for a drink, Sandy? Would you like a seat?"

She apparently only had one mode. "Aw, look at the little puppy. He doesn't know how to behave around a real dog."

"Well you're certainly that, Sandy. Pull up a pew. It's okay Martin, she's always like this."

"Nah, I've gotta scram. Running down a lead, will catch you later though."

"Like the clap." Zara muttered this last under her breath. It was nice to know she wouldn't quite stoop to Sandy's level.

A dozen relieved eyes followed Sandy's passage out of the room, on behalf of the ears attached to them. The woman seemed to carry a toxic cloud around her.

"Wow. She was... interesting."

"Damn straight. Draining, too. I try to see her in small doses, if at all."

"So, Prada, huh?"

"Er, I'm pleading the fifth."

"You're not in America."

"No, but I'm sure some proportion of Prada is, and I've apparently whored myself out to them."

"Touché." I felt strangely better after the run-in with Sandy. It was a nice distraction from the events of the morning, which Zara then brought crashing back.

"So what happened? Why did you lose your job?"

"It's complicated. I sort of quit, but then got fired."

"So you had a reasonable complaint, then?" Concise questions from Zara. The day was getting stranger.

"Reasonable means different things to different people. I think I had a good reason."

"Well it must have been something pretty critical, then. Did you catch someone with their hand in the till? My sister once caught a secretary who had managed to steal over a thousand reams of paper."

"Nothing like that, no, I would have liked a nice simple reason to be outraged. This was much more serious: it was about my photograph."

"What, they stole your personal work for the company? Shel told me you've got some interesting shots - she likes the one of the smoking clowns - but wouldn't copyright law cover you? I wouldn't expect an office contract to claim your personal work."

"Sorry, bad choice of words. They wanted to photograph me, for a new ID card scheme. RFID tags, secure entry to the office, that sort of thing."

"I'm guessing there's a point somewhere in there?" When Zara asks you for the point, you know you're waffling.

"It's everything I stand against, Zara. That level of technology lets them potentially track employees all over the building, monitor how long you're in each room."

"That's a little creepy, I suppose, but it's their office."

"By examining multiple staff members, they can see who you associate with, for how long, when and where. They can time your productivity, as they measure it, to a resolution of seconds.

"They can superficially separate a personal discussion from a business one. They can see when you use the printer, the toilet and the break room, with who and for what. They own your information, Zara, and that's a scary thought. They will know who you are, what you are doing and who you are with. And that approach always, always leads to fascism."

"Isn't that an extreme concern for an office? They say if you have nothing to hide..."

"Don't you see? It's precisely those in power who say that. If we let boundless surveillance happen in the office without protest, we normalise it. The surveillance state is terrifying precisely because it assumes as much power as is normalised. We've seen it since 9/11, we've see it since the London bombings.

"The people in power will make assumptions based on their data and act accordingly. The issue is that their assumptions are only ever correct, by definition, for the middle of the bell-curve. Where does that leave the outliers? The odd, the unusual? Why should our points of difference condemn us?

"That's leaving aside the very concept of privacy, and a right to freedom from observation, but even by itself it's the reason why I'll opt out of every data-collection trap I can, even at the cost of a job. That's my bottom line."

Zara was silent, staring at me. She looked puzzled. "Should I be worried that your rant almost made sense?"

I chuckled, "Well, that's good to hear. I was beginning to think I'd lost my job for nothing."

"So what will you do now?"

"I'm going to re-assess my biases, I think. I've shied away from the industry in the past, but I wonder if wedding photography might actually be a step up."

"Let me know if you do decide on that path - I've got a friend – Greg, I think you met at that cocktail thing – who wants an off-beat photographer for his wedding, could be a good start."

"Thanks, Zara, I'll talk to Shel and let you know."

"Good boy, it sounds like you're learning."

18 - HEAVY USERS

Shelley didn't approve of my friendship with Odd Bob. Oh, crap. I'm doing this wrong all over again. You probably want to know about my job, and I'll get there, I promise, but I need to cover more important matters first, while I remember: so Odd Bob.

"You realise he's just a homeless bum, scamming you for all he can?" She had on her patronising face - she wears that one a lot, and it pushes my buttons.

"You only think that, 'cause all you've seen is his public persona. He's a real method actor, old-school, so he won't break character to meet you properly. You've got to look past the dirt..."

"And the stench of urine."

"Yeah, like I said, he's a method actor. If he were in San Francisco, he'd be a minor celebrity around town, a truly respected performance artist."

"Then why isn't he there?"

"Because that wouldn't be enough of a challenge. He said he's enjoyed the heights of the organised theatre, and been corrupted by its excesses. He says his street performance is more sincere than any of the dreck created by corporate shills who call themselves playwrights these days."

"I take it back, he sounds really balanced."

"It's easy for you to mock him."

"Yes, it is."

"Take a moment and put yourself in his shoes, Shel."

"I'd probably catch something."

"Odd Bob helped me to define and come to terms with who I am, with how I can change the world. He's probably my, er, my second-best role model, when you get down to it."

"Well that does explain a thing or two. I'm not going to stop you from seeing him, Martin, I just wish you'd be a little bit less trusting of the man. I mean, you think taxi drivers are a distributed spy network, for God's sake, but you're bowing and scraping for someone who appears to every human sense as a disturbed transient."

"Let's not bring the taxi-drivers into this, Shel. I understand your concerns. I was suspicious at first, too – Odd Bob seemed too good to be true. But if he were here, he'd ask you, would someone dress and behave like he does, all to take advantage of a dashing young man?"

"Well if they would, then they would clearly be a dangerous and disturbing individual. Be careful, is all I'm saying, and please don't give him any more money, especially when you're only working casually yourself. If he really is your friend, he'll understand."

"I don't give him money. Well, okay, I have given him a little, a time or two, but most often I just buy him the odd cup of tea. Or a pint. Occasionally a hot meal. Honestly, I've given far more money to his friends than I have to him."

"Uhm, which friends are those?"

"While he's performing his role, he spends a lot of time with the real homeless community. He helps them out, and so do I. It's one valid use of the evil that is money."

"Well feel free to send that evil my way any time you like. I could use a hand with the rent, you know."

"I know, Shel, and I will. It's just, not this week, okay? I just paid one of Odd Bob's friends – he used to be an electrician – to disconnect a few CCTV cameras."

"Council cameras? That's illegal, Martin. What were you thinking?"

"It wasn't my idea, Shel, and Trevor, that's the electrician, he said he'd be happy for a few days in jail if he got caught, so Odd Bob thought it would be a good use of his skills."

"Then what was the money for, if Trevor wanted to do it?"

"You can't expect him to work for free, just because he's homeless. Odd Bob explained how it makes sense to pay a homeless electrician more than the going rate, and especially in a case like this, when he's taking such a risk."

"So did he do it?"

"Yep, Odd Bob said that all of the cameras down Oxford Street went offline last night. Trevor did a really smooth job, didn't even cut the lines!"

"So you're taking the word of Odd Bob both that his fellow homeless man was an electrician, and that he deactivated a suite of CCTV cameras without cutting the wires?"

"When you put it like that, it sounds stupid, but it's not a fair summary. It's Odd Bob, and I trust him. Besides, there's the prophecy." I winced even as I said it: I hadn't told Shel about the seer.

"The prophecy."

I hadn't heard that particular edge in her voice before, but decided that confidence was the best approach. "Yes, the prophecy. I visited a mystic, and she told me to beware the all-seeing eyes."

She didn't look convinced, so I launched into an account of Odd Bob's introduction to the seer.

"...So she told me about my destiny, delivered the warning, and then I left."

"So this absolutely authentic psychic, who sounds like a real charmer, by the way, told you that there was a pattern, and to beware the all-seeing eyes? That was the fifty-quid revelation from the mold-woman?"

"Don't be sarcastic, Shel, she was really into it."

"I could be really into it too, at fifty quid for five minutes."

"The money was symbolic."

"Ah, so she gave it back afterward?"

"Er, no, I think the spirits took it."

"Do you ever listen to yourself, Martin? Sometimes I wonder why I bother."

I have her my best puppy-dog expression – learned during Barnaby's house-training phase – and tried to look worldly.

She sighed. "Don't do that to your face, the wind might change, you poor, naive boy." I might have missed "worldly" by a whisker or two, but at least she didn't sound angry.

"I'll tell you your future, and I don't need a penny or a skin disease to do it: What star-sign are you?"

"What star-sign? I'm a Gemini, but I don't really go in for astrology."

"Hush. If you're prepared to listen to a fake psychic's fake predictions, then you can damn well listen to your real girlfriend's fake predictions, which are actually going to come true."

"I don't think a fake prediction can come true."

"Of course it can. Allow me to demonstrate. Look into my eyes... Deep into my eyes... The images are furious and violent, I hear screaming, oh, such screaming... I can foresee that you are about to have sex."

"Nope, not gonna happen."

"Let me try that again. You are going to have sex very soon..."

"That's cheating, Shel, and you shouldn't mock the spirits."

"You're an atheist, Martin."

"Yeah, but I keep an open mind." I muttered this, as it didn't seem a good time to start another argument.

"Anyway, I wasn't mocking the spirits, but I am now: Oh great and perverted spirits, please enjoy the show. Introducing the main attraction, as unlikely as that might be: Martin. Watch in awe as I fuck his brains out."

"Not funny... Not... Hey, okay... Let me..."

"Ssh, Martin, that's it, you know what to do. Let the spirits watch in peace... "

19 - AMBITION

Learning to treat photography as an occupation was new and exciting. For me, anyway. Shelley had a few things to say about it.

"I don't understand what you want from life, Martin. I understand your whole passive-aggressive approach to the system, but I don't know what you want it to achieve. Where does it all lead?"

"You don't get it at all, then, Shel, if you think it's just me being difficult. It's about a holistic approach to injustice and inequality. People are encouraged to think of others, of problems with the system, of ways to improve the world, only in little, carefully orchestrated blocks." She looked set to interrupt, but I pushed on.

"Take voting, for example. The electoral system is heavily advertised and promoted as our chance to exercise a free choice of our preferred government. Yet, if our preference lies completely outside those boundaries, then we have no room for engagement. It's an entirely inflexible system, disguised as a choice."

I paused for breath, and she jumped in.

"I'm gonna stop you there, Martin. What the hell does the electoral system have to do with what happened at Greg and Reshma's wedding?"

"I was getting there, Shel. "

"Well get there faster. I'm dying to know."

"The issue is that dominant powers spend a lot of the country's money to guarantee a certain level of apathy towards political change."

"You didn't take a single photo of the bride. Not. One. Single. Shot."

"That's not true - I captured her walking down the aisle."

"From behind. At a ridiculously-low angle."

"I thought I'd call that one *Into Slavery* - it fits the sexist vows they used perfectly. My vision is about changing the paradigm, undermining and countering the dominant modes of society."

"It was her wedding day, Martin, and from behind doesn't count: you didn't actually photograph her. No number of buzzwords are going to fix that."

"You're talking around the issue, Shel, this is the heart of what I believe."

"But you don't have the right to impose it on somebody else's wedding."

"I had the responsibility! They said they wanted an off-beat view of the wedding, and that's what I gave them."

"You took two dozen shots of a vagrant sleeping outside the church, shot the gift table to make it look like a looming omen, and let's not forget that delightful sequence of the best man picking his nose then wiping it on his suit tails."

"The homeless man wasn't sleeping - he was moving under

the blanket, and smiling. I thought it was appropriate: he was just wringing what pleasure he could from this world, as were the happy couple."

Shelley snorted and looked upset, so I quickly continued.

"It illustrates the different social strata and the identical desires that underpin them. I call the sequence *different strokes*, and I can guarantee nobody else will have wedding photos like those."

"Some would say that's a good thing. You can't just go around educating people against their will. I'm not saying your ideas are wrong – not at the moment, anyway – but you need to find appropriate channels for your crusade.

"If you really want political change, why not create your own party, or run as an independent, and make your very election platform about changing the system? Wouldn't that be better than faffing about with your bloody camera?"

"There's more to it than that. This is the heart of what I believe: power wants to sustain and nurture power, and actions to ensure survival of a system that is prioritising your desires are simply logical, if the system allows them. Where do our tax dollars go?"

"Well, I don't think Greg is planning on paying you for the wedding shots, so you're not going to have any tax dollars to speak of."

"You know what I mean. Sure, a certain proportion does go to roads, hospitals and other essential services, but a substantial amount is allocated to so-called cultural features and events. Sports fields, parks, concerts, orchestras, theatre, all designed with one common purpose in mind: the distraction and assimilation of the middle class."

"Oh, come on Martin, you go to the theatre. And you're always talking about that awful homeless man and what a great actor he is."

"Leave Odd Bob out of this, he's not part of the system. I go to the theatre precisely because the illusion is effective: even knowing how it operates, I'm not immune to its charms. I realise that it's a weakness, and I try to avoid the temptation, but it is simply a pervasive, compulsive approach, and damn it, it works. I'm just glad I have the fortitude not to vote."

"Well done you."

"Don't be sarcastic, Shel, you're just parroting their propaganda. Active participation in a game you know is rigged is nothing short of stupid."

"Well call me stupid, then, but I won't be the one sleeping on the couch tonight."

"Er, I didn't mean you."

"You don't know what you meant. You don't know where you're going at all. I can help with the next steps, though: you're going to write an apology to Greg and Reshma. Here, I'll dictate..."

The worst part is that she was right. I had Odd Bob's teachings and my philosophy of life, but I was treading water, at best.

I needed a push to give me some momentum.

20 - ODD LEAVINGS

Odd Bob was a good friend, the best of friends, really. It was hard to lose him like I did, and even more of a loss for the city.

Few actors manage to be wholly committed to both their craft and to a cause. Most focus on one, to the detriment of the other. While there's nothing wrong with an actor advocating for lost children – not *for* the loss of children, you understand, but against it – feeding the hungry or sharing their political inclination with others, their true passion will always be evident, and that is often to the stage.

Odd Bob managed to achieve them seamlessly: he was actor and activist both, with the entirety of his being.

It takes an activist and an actor both to die the way he did, which is probably just as well.

He did fortify himself for that final performance - I had lent him a little money the day before, and he had spent some of it on a top-shelf bottle of whiskey. It was found, drained, near the station platform.

Perhaps the alcohol immersed him too fully in his role, for he stood there, a lopped-off branch in his hand, as an express train approached, straddling the tracks with a scowl on his face.

He looked radiant, a witness said, although she was herself high as a kite at 7.00 in the morning.

His last words were loud, solidly delivered, and if his voice were not optimal for the role, at least he tried.

"You shall not pass," rang out clearly across the station, and the same witness swore that the train hesitated for a split second, before passing in a violent squeal of brakes.

Odd Bob was scattered down the Paddington-Heathrow Line, in full view of no less than three of his despised cameras.

Now that I think back, I can't figure out what he was doing over that side of London. Or why he would ignore, and even contravene, his own stand against the CCTV plague.

"Stand against" was an unfortunate choice of words, but you get the idea; I'd like to think that his final act meant something. Something other than too much Scotch and a newfound belief in magic.

There was no funeral. Odd Bob had no property, no will, no descendents or acknowledged family. I went to his favourite alleyway, and said a few words. They weren't great words, but they were better than the "kook challenges train" approach adopted by the tabloids. I kept the tone light, but solemn, as the great man would have liked.

I could still smell him in the alleyway, so I didn't stay long. If there was one thing Odd Bob was good at, it was disturbing people.

I dreamed, that night, of the pattern we had searched for. Maybe that was all it was when the tallies were counted: a dream of a solution, a foul stench in a vacant alleyway, an echo in lesser minds.

I woke weeping for my lost friend, and resolved to carry on his legacy. Not the acting, there was no way I was going into that terrifying world, but the advocacy, the activism. I could never be an Odd Bob, but perhaps I could be Martin, changer of the world.

21 - OF LITTLE CONSEQUENCE

"So, you see the papers this morning?"

"Who still reads the papers?"

"Don't be so fucking difficult. Did you read the news?"

"Be more specific in your questions, then, and save us both some time. Yeah, I read the news, what of it?"

"Did you catch the old man on the train tracks story?"

"Oh, yeah, that was fuckin' hilarious. You shall not.... Splosh!"

"Bit of respect, mate, that was Odd Bob."

"Odd Bob? Doesn't ring a bell."

"Oh come off it, you know Odd Bob. He's the old beggar, always hanging 'round Turnpike Lane."

"Aw, that's just shitty. I didn't know his name, but kinda liked the old con-man, so long as you stood upwind. Did you ever hear his acting routine?"

"Is that the one where he went off about being a master thespian? Nailed it every time, I wonder if he could have been, in another life?"

"I doubt it, a voice like that. He did have a presence, though, I'll give him that."

"Yeah, that he did."

"Hey, was he involved in this whole mess we're dealing with?"

"Nah, I doubt it."

"You sure? He's just the kind of operative I'd send in."

"Nope, brass would've told us if they had another player. He was just what he seemed: a boozy old drunk, who went out in style."

"Ah, more's the pity. To Old Bob, I hope you're still laughing about your exit on the other side. And that the hangover isn't too bad."

"That's Odd Bob, but I like the toast."

22 - ON THE INSIDE

One thing you learn early on is when to take a stand. Like so many other lessons, I got it wrong a time or two. Filming state brutality, or leaking evidence of corruption are worthwhile causes. Arguing with a parking warden about your magnet scheme until the police are called is not.

I won't say I've done time. Well, I have, but it wasn't that dramatic. Three hours on the inside. Well, the police holding cell, but it was still imprisonment, even if you sugar-coat it.

I sat in the crowded cell, alongside men and women who'd been picked up for all sorts of unspeakable crimes. Admittedly, most seemed to be drunk and disorderly, but I'm sure there were some hardened criminals scattered amongst us.

One woman wanted to talk to me, even seemed friendly. That told me that she was a mole, placed there to gain information about my ideology. I refused to speak to her, and she soon gave up. Spies aren't built like in the movies: they've got as little patience and competence as the rest of us.

When I was released, they returned my belongings. I looked carefully through the contents of my wallet, searching for bugs, but couldn't find anything out of place. I was certain some of my magnets were missing, but it didn't seem the time or place to make a fuss.

I decided to burn the wallet when I got home, just to be safe. Shelley intervened only after I had located a suitable pot and a book of matches.

"But Shel, eternal vigilance is the price of liberty. Eternal vigilance and the odd accessory."

"I'm sure that's a valuable addendum to the party line, but you're not burning your wallet. Besides, isn't eternal vigilance the very thing you're so worried about?"

"That's a deliberate misinterpretation. There's a difference between vigilance and snooping."

"Don't explain it to me now, I'm still coming to terms with your magnet scheme. You don't even drive."

Isn't it a bit arrogant, you may wonder, to believe the powers-that-be would send a spy after me? It would be, and more than a little, without some context.

I don't believe the government is watching me. I believe they're watching *everyone*.

Odd Bob explained it like this: we hold the true power of numbers, we just don't ever wield it in any meaningful way. They know this – it's one of the constants of any system of government – so they must watch us all, ever alert for anomalies who could forge a weapon of the people, show them their true potential.

The reason they'd send a spy for me, but not for you, is simple: I'm a digital ghost, a phantom.

In the past year, at least prior to my arrest, I'd appeared on London's ubiquitous CCTV network precisely once, and I was wearing a baseball cap at the time and facing away from the lens. I don't have a Facebook page, Tweet, Instagram, Vine or otherwise engage with social media. I avoid civic buildings and other locations where the surveillance state has triumphed. I have a cellphone, but it's an outdated Nokia, lacking GPS and other "smart" features, and I usually leave it at home.

I do play online games, to my eternal benefit, but I always do so through a proxy, and the information I provide is deliberately misleading. Shelley *could* have been an agent, looking to entrap me, but I took a risk in her case, and it paid off.

I could blend in, disguise myself better by creating misleading profiles online. I could populate a Facebook page with photos and *like* a hundred random brands. But it's a line I draw: I will not be a willing cog in the advertising culture, I will not whore myself out to corporate interests.

Well, not again: my short-lived cubicle career was enough.

When you've got a well-oiled structure, an opt-in feast of personal information, freely shared, it suddenly makes sense to use more direct means to corral the ghosts. There aren't many of us, and we're easily located: in London, just go where the cameras aren't.

23 - WATCHER BACK

The iris scanner thought for a moment, electrons whirling around its complex circuitry in momentary indecision, before it beeped its consent, committed to the choice, and the door slid smoothly open.

She shuffled inside, trying to maintain the confident posture she had cultivated. The waiting eyes were not friendly. "Sir. Ma'am."

"You're late, agent."

"Sorry, sir." She knew excuses were neither wanted nor appreciated here.

"And you failed in your mission."

"Yes, ma'am."

"Debrief us, please."

This, she could do. "The target appeared receptive at first approach, but became suspicious when social niceties were applied. He then rejected any further attempts at interaction, and remained motivated by suspicion for the remainder of the encounter."

"Please elaborate on the social niceties attempted." The joint chief's face was granite, his tone not much softer.

"Fleeting eye contact, slight increase in facial blood flow, contraction of facial muscles to produce an upward curve to the lips. Generic greeting number two followed by the adoption of receptive posture twelve-b."

"And the target's specific reaction?" The female chief's voice was soft, almost gentle, but her eyes were harder still than her colleague's, her face carved flat from years of metaphorical poker.

"The target's facial expression initially indicated warmth and greeting, but became studiously blank after contact was initiated. While untrained, the subject appeared to have excellent impulse control, and refused to engage in level two interactions, either verbal or non. Despite the target's evident control, microexpressions indicating fear and contempt were repeatedly visible during the attempted engagement."

"Thank you, agent. It is evident that a direct solution is out of the question for this subject. Did you have anything else to add?

"Yes sir, ma'am, I, er, took the liberty of replacing his wallet lining with one from R&D. It can be activated with a directional wave, and will pick up conversions within earshot." She shuddered inwardly while awaiting the response. Initiative was a useful asset for a spy, but too much could eventually be fatal, and the old guard weren't always keen on the use of gadgets.

"That will be all, thank you agent." No smile, but no reprimand, either.

She left the room quickly, allowing relief to flash over her own face as the door closed decisively behind her.

24 - WHAT IFS

Since I lost Odd Bob, I've been almost paranoid. Maybe his death was some misguided sacrifice to his cause, a blameless tragedy, but it's more likely the faceless *they* had something to do with it, and I can't help but feel more on edge than ever.

To avoid the creeping sensation that my world is spiralling out of control, I take refuge in baby names.

We don't have any children, unless you count the dog, or plans to have any, but an age of autocorrect makes this worth worrying about, on behalf of any future pregnancies.

When Payton becomes Patron in any standard dictionary, what if you make an incorrect choice? What if Beatrice becomes Bitch, or Whitney becomes Whitey? So much potential for harm in an electronic world.

A thousand names, a thousand words, swimming around in my head, pricking my worries and piquing my interest. I feel them even now, the peripheral pluralities of possibility, alliterating my anxieties into jagged lines of simple text.

At times, they seem to join the pattern, insignificant components that somehow represent the whole, but I cannot grasp these volatile thoughts, can not hold them still long enough for my eyes to bring them swimming into focus.

It may be needless worrying, but at least it's a good distraction from the larger concerns of this perilous world – and I'm not going to be detained for picking a baby name. Not yet, anyway.

They used to call us crazy. Many still do, in fact. Whistleblowers like Manning and Snowden can confirm our long-held belief that power will be abused and privacy will be invaded, but most people remain focused on continuing their subjugation to large corporate structures: paying the mortgage, buying the groceries, and committing petty fraud on their tax returns.

When I talk to her, I often get upset. She's smart, probably smarter than me, and passionate, but I can't seem to ignite that passion into a flame with purpose. Instead, she unleashes it at the late bus, the missed concert, at me.

She's my everything, my world, and yet it sometimes feels like we inhabit different worlds. She walks down Oxford Street, sees shoes and bags and pretty delights that she would never waste money on. I walk beside her, seeing boldly-traced lines of corruption and compromise, distractions and illusions stitched large across vivid red leather facades. Inside those beautifully labelled bags, nothing but crumpled sheets of paper as blank as the promise of the storefronts.

I wondered when they would get to me. Would it be the government men and women, all politeness and acronyms and black SUVs? More likely low-level hirelings with non-specific European accents and no records.

There is a shortage of plumbers in most civilised countries these days, and it's because nobody likes to get their hands dirty. I assume thugs are in similar short supply, or would be if police departments didn't offer such an attractive career for them.

Contemplating my eventual fate may seem morbid, and

probably was. But it passed the time until I could be with her again.

I arrived home, and she was gone. I searched the flat, looking for a note, a reason. No messages on my phone. The dog, gone too, his leash missing.

I knew, then, that she'd been kidnapped.

"But wait!" you might ask, "Hasn't she just taken the dog for a walk?" That's what they would want me to think. She knows how worried I get. She would have left a note. They've been monitoring me since they got to Odd Bob, and finally identified a subversive element.

"Er, why would they take the dog?" You may logically follow.

The reason is simple, if too unpleasant for civilised consideration: It's much safer to threaten harm to an animal than a human. The torture of an animal has fewer potential repercussions, and pet owners are easy to manipulate with their animal's life on the line.

They'll be asking her about my credo, investigating my life by proxy, before deciding whether to detain me indefinitely.

So, it turned out that she was walking the dog, after all. This time.

25 - WE WATCH THE WATCHERS

"Can you see them?"

"See who?"

"The targets, you muppet."

"No need to get snippy. Don't you think I'd tell you if I'd seen them?"

"I never know with you."

"Well, that's easy for... wait. There they are, the girl and the dog."

"Sure it's the right pair?"

"Big, stupid-looking dog, a little bit twitchy?"

"Ignore the dog, fucktard. What does the girl look like?"

"Oh. She's slim, shortish dark hair, five-foot-seven or eight, part Asian by the look of her."

"Glasses?"

"Yeah, black, thick plastic rims. Too geeky for my liking."

"It's her. Radio the go team and give the okay."

"On it. Here, you take over the scope. Bravo team, this is Alpha, do you copy? Over."

"We copy, Alpha, Bravo ready to roll. Over."

"Shh - wait. They're turning around. Looks like she's forgotten something."

"Bravo, stand by. Over."

"Copy that, Alpha. Over."

"Shit. They're entering the apartment building. Tell Bravo to stand down. We'll lose our window."

"Stand down, Bravo. I repeat, stand down. Over."

"Why are we collecting them, anyway? And why the dog? Did it witness something?"

"Fucked if I know. We're just following orders."

"Too much of that going round these days, if you ask me."

"I didn't. The job's off for today, anyway, so you can make your own decisions for the afternoon. Go on little Ted, run through a field, be free."

"Sarcasm is the last resort of the... Hey, is that them coming back out?"

"Yeah, but we can't hit them now: we'd get caught up in the after-school traffic. Nothing worse than a "guest" moaning and squirming in the back of your van through a traffic jam, and that's without a dog along for the ride."

"Sounds like there's a little latitude with those orders after all, huh? Want to grab a coffee?"

"Be careful how you talk about the orders: for the record, our approved *go-time closed at 14.50, and she re-emerged at 14.51. Can't grab a drink today, it's my daughter's second birthday, and I've still got to pick up the cake."*

"Ah, the joys of parenthood. Some other time, then?"

"Sure thing, Ted, see you tomorrow."

"Later."

26 - TRIVIAL PURSUITS

We often fight. Well, 'fight' isn't the right word. We argue. At least it's not one-sided, even if she usually wins.

"Thank God you're home, Shel. And Barnaby, too. Come here, boy. Who's a good dog?"

"Um, is something wrong, Martin?"

"I thought you'd been kidnapped!"

"Again? You worry about that every time I take him for a walk."

"But I noticed a mark on the building today, two little pink dots."

"Okay... I hope you can explain that, or I'm going to run you down to the hospital."

"Haven't you seen the emails? Small spots of paint are used to mark houses with dogs in them, then the dogs get taken."

"And how exactly is that supposed to work for our apartment?"

"I'm just saying we should be careful with Barnaby."

"Who would want to steal Barnaby? He looks like he's got Tourettes, the way he twitches."

"Don't be mean, he can hear you. You're a good, perfect dog, aren't you boy. I thought they must have taken both of you."

"So you're suggesting that there's a major criminal network, coordinated across the city, to kidnap dogs, and they'd also take the owner on a whim."

"Not just across the city. I've seen emails from around the world."

"Do you ever listen to yourself, Martin?"

"It's not crazy – I've seen the photos."

"Let me guess. One person's dog was stolen, and that person noticed some markings on their fence. They put two and two together, someone else who had lost a dog noticed a marking on their own fence, and a legend was born."

"Well, yes, but plenty more people have seen the markings, and odd characters watching their dogs." I could hear my voice getting higher as I tried to explain what I knew, and struggled to control it.

"It's a completely fallacious argument, though. Correlation does not imply causation."

"What do you mean? A pattern is a pattern."

"Yes, but this isn't a pattern. This is a couple of third-party anecdotes that make a spurious statistical connection, then extrapolate it as a fact."

"Anecdotes are more important than statistics, though – we aren't numbers."

"Anecdotes are important, yes, but only when they refer to our own experience. They are never evidence, because evidence refers to more objective metrics, one example of which can be statistics, abused as they often are.

"In this case, it is also a ridiculous link, even if you allow the anecdotes priority. In any given city, there is senseless graffiti, there are odd fungi and other phenomena that can cause markings on a fence, from a wheelbarrow or car brushing against it, to a neighbour's weed spray affecting the wood.

"Unless your anecdotes include a trio of criminals carefully painting the fence, before their known associates arrive later to collect the dog, it's just an insane viewpoint."

"Buu.."

"Let me finish. Why would any criminal risk exposure once to mark the fence, then a second time to collect the dog? And why, if it were true, would this behaviour persist long after the urban legend has become so widespread?

"If *I* were behind such a conspiracy, I'd have switched from fences to letterboxes, chalk marks on the sidewalk, or marking the houses in a private online map."

"It's just a theory. I didn't say I believed it, just that it made me nervous."

"It's not a theory, it's inexcusable stupidity, but I'm glad you're backing off it now."

There are two things that she means to me, above all others. She takes me more or less seriously, when anyone else would laugh, would turn away in embarrassment. And she has a nice arse. I mean it, a really firm, round bottom, that just sits comfortably on my lap.

Okay, just kidding about the arse - although you should check it out (don't, I'm the jealous type) – it's her own passion that really draws me in. She'll claim that I'm exaggerating, that she's a pessimist at heart, but once you've seen those fires flare up in her eyes, it's undeniable.

We get set into routines, all too often in this life. Our nights seem to cry out for organisation, for structure, so we package them up neatly: movie night, pasta night, TV night, sex night. We don't get assimilated: we assimilate, taking the steady progression of unchallenged normalcy into ourselves, until it becomes as dull and mundane as we feel, and then we die.

That's the pessimistic view, anyway. We can, and should, challenge this tendency, but it doesn't have to be an epic battle. Once a week, or even a month, shake the plans up a bit. Put on a movie on TV night. Go out for an unplanned walk. Invite friends along on an outing, although probably not to sex night.

For us, it's the arguments that keep us fresh and vibrant. Difficult as they may in the immediate moment, they have brought us closer together than anything else.

It was fitting, then, that an argument brought us so close to the truth of the pattern.

27 - SIMULATION SITUATION?

"Do you ever wonder if this is all an illusion, a simulation, whether we're just little brains living in tanks somewhere, experiencing this life that doesn't really exist?"

"No."

"Seriously, Shel - how can you tell that this is real?"

"You can't tell that this is real, but it has all the hallmarks of being real. From my perspective, which you're so keen on as the be-all and end-all, this is reality, and there's no point positing another for which I can never have any evidence. As far as I'm concerned at this moment, this is real life."

"And it doesn't bother you?"

"No. Why would it bother me? Yes, there's an outside possibility that this could be defined as a simulation..."

"Not just an outside possibility. Our experience can be defined as the way our brains subjectively collate the information of our senses – that fits a decent concept of simulation."

"No it doesn't, mister. Simulation is a projected scenario, with a set of parameters that model a situation, event or process. Our senses are more analogous to robotic sensors, and our brain the processor that converts their feedback to usable information. Organisms operate to an extent like machines, not at all like simulations."

"I'm just saying, what if our brains are being fed incorrect data? What if it's all some big experiment? What if this world isn't reality?"

"As far as I'm concerned, it is. If this world were simply some 1s and 0s, some words on a page, I'd like to put in an official request for an upgrade. If some being, some force, is putting in the effort to create a world for me, I think a squat in London is a little shoddy, don't you? How about *Pride and Prejudice* as a backdrop, or at least *Downton Abbey*?"

"I hate it when you patronise me. I'm going to bed."

"I hate it when you act like a tosser and refuse to turn that critical eye on your own assumptions. You're going to the sofa."

For the record, she was joking about the sofa. But she did claim most of the duvet.

28 - OR PERHAPS NOT

"Sir, we've lost another one."

"Another what?"

"Another agent, sir."

"Shit. Is it asking too much, Brigadier, or could you for once make a full report without requiring me to reach over and tear the words from your mouth?"

"Er, yes sir. Sorry sir."

"Three-bags-full sir, I'm sure. Out with it."

"The operative was code-named Odd Bob, a former special-forces man, medical discharge four years ago, when he joined our deep cover team. A real stand-up chap, sir."

"I'm familiar with the man, Trent. What were his operation status and circumstance of death?"

"Operation in progress, Sir, he hadn't reported back with a current status in some time, but that's the nature of deep cover work."

"Thank you Brigadier, I'm familiar with the nature of deep cover work. Please skip the drivel and continue."

"Of course, sir. Agent Odd Bob was attempting to dissuade the target with a truth bomb."

"Now that technique I'm not aware of. Please elaborate."

"Yes sir. It's something our labs came up with, a joint project with US intel, I think. The process involves taking the classified facts of the matter, then couching them in an obnoxious and ridiculous manner and handing them to the target.

"The classic example is the joke gift of condoms to parents with five children. A large box is handed over, with a light-hearted message, and the incongruity of the condoms amuses the recipients, who might otherwise take offense if the same giver simply suggests that they use a condom in the future."

"Hmm, sounds like an interesting theory, although the example is a little weak."

"It is, sir, but even that 'soft' example worked in 99.5% of cases. They ran a long-term study, using thousands of large families as a sample set.

"A better, if unvalidated study, is the use of urban legend websites to demonstrate how ridiculous certain theories are. We start with the patently absurd theories, of course, and then link the more accurate conspiracies and urban legends to those. The truth is posted right there, in plain sight, then it's brutally mocked and "critiqued" using such convoluted logic that few will consider the original claim seriously. For most, it's just another debunked bit of information, not worth worrying about or pursuing.

"In the present case, Odd Bob was required to give Martin confirmation of his fears and concerns, delivered by a urine-soaked alcoholic who was clearly scamming him for money. Odd Bob even introduced a deranged homeless companion as a 'psychic', to really seal the deal. Nobody could have done it better, Sir, it was a masterful truth bomb."

"So his death was unrelated, then?"

"Er, the circumstances of his death are still under investigation, sir. The official cover story is that he stood on some train tracks, playing Gandalf, and the train refused to play along."

"That's creative, Brigadier."

"Not really, sir, it's another truth bomb, my own idea, this time."

"Are you saying that a highly trained operative killed himself in front of a train?"

"While drunk, holding a staff and spouting lines from Tolkien, yes sir."

"And you're certain it had no bearing on his mission?"

"Yes sir, how could it? We'll be hard-pressed to see another truth bomb as effective as Agent Odd Bob's. Martin will be further from any volatile knowledge than ever before."

"I wish I shared your optimism, soldier. I want you to step up observation of Martin, with a capture order on standby for the girl. And keep ears on them too. Is he still avoiding the cameras?"

"Yes, sir, the visible ones."

"Good. At least we'll know where to find him. I want word immediately if there are any sudden changes to his behaviour. Understood?"

"Yes sir."

"Thank you, Brigadier - sincerely, this time. Dismissed."

29 - FISH BOWL

It was only last week, but it feels like an eternity ago. I talked to Shelley, argued, really, then we made up, made love and went to sleep: a normal Tuesday evening.

That moment of drifting to sleep marks my last normal memory, the definitive line between then and now.

I woke up the next morning, and immediately felt the change. Someone was watching me. Shelley was still asleep, snoring softly beside me. Barnaby was whining at the front door, waiting to be let outside, and nobody else was in our apartment. Except they were. This wasn't that vague tingling between the shoulder-blades that sometimes afflicts all of us; this was real.

I could feel the intruders sliding their eyes over our slightly-ripe sheets, the rise of Shelley's body beneath its peaks and troughs, lingering on the cup collection beside the bed, collating and critiquing the details of our room, of our lives. I was suddenly conscious of my own bed-hair, of the taste of sour morning breath and an intense need to visit the water closet.

The eyes followed me everywhere. Do you know how invasive it is, sitting on the toilet and feeling anonymous strangers leering at you? How frustrating it is to not even know in which direction to flip them off? Children raised in religious families have probably experienced this – or at least a shadow of it – when introduced to the theological concept of omnipotence, but this was no benevolent supreme being.

So I shat quietly and quickly, trying to keep my bathroom habits as "normal" as possible. When people are watching, you examine everything well beyond the point of paranoia.

What is the normal way to wipe your arse? Left hand or right? Sitting, standing or somewhere in between? Front to back or back to front? Folding or crushing? Wet or dry paper? And don't get me started on hand-washing or showering. My nether regions have never been so well-scrubbed, using so many different techniques in pursuit of the normal.

I tried to conjure up ways to entrap the eyes, to think like a private investigator, which was difficult. I've never met one in real life, and it's hard to emulate a fictitious gumshoe without a substantial alcohol dependency.

Sans also fedora, trench coat and leads, I decided to work with what I knew: photography. I scoured folders of my work, thousands of images I'd been meaning to sort out and process, looking for a sign of the watchers.

If they really were out there, if I wasn't losing my mind – and the possibility did occur to me, about once per minute – then there must be a trace. But the photos didn't hold it.

I even took my camera, fitted a nice 16mm wide-angle lens, and took a handful of panoramic shots in the apartment, the street and the park. All they revealed were the apartment, the street and the park. I zoomed in to pixel level, inverted the colours and even ran face-detection macros, but my pictures remained stubbornly watcher-free.

Yet still they watched.

The watching also made romance near-impossible. My mind was so consumed with looking out for the unseen audience that I couldn't focus on a word she was saying, not really, and I couldn't tell her what I was preoccupied with, because then they would know I was on to them.

It was a dry week, that's for sure.

Shelley couldn't have missed my preoccupation, but she didn't act as if anything was unusual. One week on, I got almost used to the ever-presence of the eyes, and began to relax my guard. That was probably part of their plan, but it's only possible to stay on edge for so long.

30 - DOES HE KNOW?

"Do you think he knows we're watching him?"

"Don't be stupid — nobody's that crazy."

"I dunno..."

"That's the litany of your life, isn't it? I dunno, I dunno. Well wise up, buddy — I know, and I'm telling you he has no idea."

"It's just... is it really crazy if we are watching him?"

"This is why you leave the thinking to me, shit-for-brains: I'm telling you he's ignorant."

"If you say so. We betting on their next argument?"

"Only if you want to bet on him. It doesn't take a superior intellect to detect a pattern, and she's got him pretty-well whipped."

"Guess not, then."

"Say, what did you do before this, anyway?"

"Um, are we allowed to talk about that?"

"Fucked if I know! I don't think we're technically allowed to talk about anything but the job, but nobody's watching us."

"Heh, yeah, I suppose that's true. I used to be a parking warden."

"You? A cunt?"

"I'm sorry?"

"You heard me: a cunt. Lowest of the low, parking wardens. What the hell did you do to get into this gig?"

"You can't just throw out that word and then continue."

"Oh, I'm sorry, did you want me to elaborate? Okay then: there's this rancid old man, hasn't bathed in months..."

"What the hell?"

"Shut the fuck up; you asked. This old man, he lives in his own filth, and every night he fucks a goat that he's tied up in a corner of his yard. When he gets done with the fucking, he cuddles up to Nelly — that's the goat's name — and he falls asleep.

"Nelly can't stand the smell of the old man, but he's tied up, right, so he just has to stand there while the perverted old coot snores away, feeling the fluids still oozing from his violated body.

"Nelly wishes, in his limited goaty way, for death. He's low, almost as low as you can get. But even Nelly the goat, given the choice, wouldn't trade places with a fucking parking warden: that would be beneath him."

"Jesus."

"Now I condensed it down for you, kept it simple: parking wardens are cunts. But if you want me to compare and contrast further, I'm sure I can..."

"No... no. I get the point. I'm gonna be sick, but I get the point. You don't like parking wardens."

"I'd take that as an understatement, but I'm glad you got free of that dirty industry. Now hand me the binoculars. I think his girl's about to take a shower."

31 - IT'S MY PARTY

Shelley sometimes makes life really difficult. Planning her surprise party, for instance.

"I just want to know where you were. Is that so much to ask?" She flounced across the room, glaring at me.

"Trust is the foundation of any relationship, Shel." Her glare darkened.

"Don't quote me at me, Martin. Of course I trust you. I just don't trust you not to be taken advantage of. Between all your waifs and strays, I want to make sure you haven't been out giving away our possessions to some random crazy." She watched my face, looking for a tell, but I wasn't going to give her one.

"I haven't Shel, of course I haven't. Can we leave it at that?" Fat chance, but I had to try.

"No, we damn well can't just leave it at that. I know you're planning something. Is it dangerous?" She hates surprise parties, so it probably was.

"It could be, in a certain light, but it's the right thing to do."

"Oh God, you're not planning another exhibition, are you? Or some warped kind of revolution?" Her lip twisted like a slug on salt.

"I can't say any more, but you'll see when the time comes."

"That's what freaks me out, Martin. Your head is a weird and very occasionally wonderful place, but you could be plotting an assassination or leading a coup, for all I know."

"You know me better than that. If I were planning to overthrow the system, it wouldn't be using those tired old models."

"I knew it. A bloody revolution. If that's what you're doing, you can count me out." She actually stamped her foot. So cute, but I was careful not to smile.

"Please, Shel, it's not what you think. I don't want to lie to you, and I think you'll like it, really. Can you just wait a couple of days?" I lowered my eyes, trying for my Barnaby special look.

"No. I'd like you to tell me right now." I guess he'd peed on the rug again.

"I, I can't. I promised someone that I'd keep it secret." This was true – Zara had an obsession with surprise parties, and had sworn us all to keep it from Shel.

"Who?" She looked ready to hunt them down.

"Someone else who you trust. That's all I can say. Just give me two days, Shel, and I promise you won't be upset."

"We'll see about that, but you're not getting a day more. Now get over here and rub my feet."

32 - SOUNDS LIKE OURS

"Hey. Psst. PSSST!"

"Wha... What the hell, man? Stop poking me!"

"Ssh! Quietly! They were talking."

"Wow. You woke me up for another lecture on the exploitation of the chimney sweeps' union?"

"No, dickwad. They were talking about his plan."

"About fuckin' time. What is it?"

"What is what?"

"The plan."

"I don't know. They were talking about it, but they didn't go into detail, and then they started whispering. It sounds like it's happening soon, whatever it is."

"Did you phone it in?"

"Are you insane? Do you know how many agencies are listening in on the cell networks?"

"Fine, sorry, I'm still half-asleep. Encrypted radio?"

"And that bloody retro code-book. They're playing this one close to the chest. The boss wants to see us for a full debrief."

"What, usual location?"

"Nah, I said 'full debrief'."

"Aw, crap. That mean head office?"

"Yep. All the way down."

"Just what I wanted. Couldn't you have let me sleep a bit longer?"

"Well, I thought you might want to see this before we head in."

"See what?"

"On the monitor, man. They're doing it."

"Ah, okay, that is worth waking up for, thanks pal."

"That's what partners are for."

33 - RUN DICK, RUN!

"Gentlemen, lady. We hoped it wouldn't come to this.

"I've called you here today to discuss the Martin situation. We've had a number of our top people monitoring it..."

"Monitoring it? Why not just put a bullet in his head and be done with it?"

"Clyde, was that you? I'll remind you that this may be a secure room, but we do not speak in such... dramatic... terms. As you may recall from your own investigation, there are, er, mitigating circumstances that make a direct approach, such as the one you've so eloquently advocated, undesirable."

"Mitigating my arse. I still say to just shoot the bastard."

"Right. If that's all you've got to say on the matter, Clyde, I suggest you leave the room."

"You can't talk to me like that, you slimy little worm. Just 'cause you ain't got the balls to do what needs to be done."

"Sidney? Yes, be a dear and shoot Clyde in the head. Quietly, if you please. Now where was I?

"Oh yes, the Martin situation. No, Sidney, just drag the body outside and dump it. Most hideous thing, isn't it? But as for Martin, I believe we were discussing the late Clyde's most straightforward idea.

"No, I believe a more subtle approach is in order. As you can see, it's not a question of stomach — or testicular fortitude, as poor departed Clyde put it — it's a much more fundamental concern.

"Our existence as a successful organisation, our ability to operate as we do, hinges on Martin's knowledge of and reaction to us, and that is an equilibrium we have every interest in maintaining. In fact, we do have a concrete plan to make the arrangement more, shall we say, rigid.

"It has been pointed out that Martin has recently come alarmingly close to a number of our initiatives. Of course, our misinformation campaign worked beautifully — thank you for that, Trish — and most people consider Martin a mere crackpot, but a number of his closer acquaintances are developing an unhealthy interest in our world.

"If you turn to page seven of the strategy document in front of you, you will see a draft road-map for turning this situation to our advantage..."

34 - ABDUCTION

"There she is. We're ready to go."

"Are you certain this time?"

"Of course I'm certain. She's alone, it's dark, what could possibly go wrong?"

"Some idiot always has to ask that question. She could scream. She could duck inside a random building. A cop or concerned citizen could intervene. Our car could break down..."

"Okay, okay, I get it. Shouldn't we be moving?"

"Not yet. She's coming toward us."

"Okay, so what do we do?"

"Just shut your mouth and wait."

"Excuse me, Miss?"

"Yes?"

"I was wondering if you'd be interested in taking a short five-minute survey?"

"Er, no thank you. I'm rushing to an appointment."

"At seven-thirty in the evening?"

"Yes. It's, um, a late-night dentist. And I don't have to explain myself to you."

"Actually, you do. Can you get in the van-Oof! Bitch! Grab her, Sid. I'll show you what I do to ungrateful whores who - Urgh! Sid! Hurry the fuck up!"

35 - DANGEROUS GAMES

"Welcome, Miss Shelley."

"Mmmmrgh."

"Yes, you will notice that you're currently gagged. That is for the protection of our people, but we apologise, regardless. Your victim from earlier had to have a dozen stitches, and we wanted to avoid a repeat of that... unpleasantness."

"Mrgh."

"Well, as the sedative wears off, you'll notice that you're also cuffed to the chair. We'll remove the gag once you promise not to bite anyone else."

"Mphh Gnu."

"I'll take that as agreement. Sidney, the gag?"

"I'll kill you, you fuckers. Biting will be the least of it. And I'll kill you last. You have no right to..."

"I appreciate the sentiment, really I do, Miss Shelley, but you're the one with no rights now. You are a guest of our little facility until you have satisfactorily answered all of our questions."

"Questions? You kidnapped me, bundled me into a van and drugged me, all for some fucking survey?"

"No, Miss Shelley, perhaps the drugs are causing you difficulty thinking. It would be unthinkable for a market research company to abduct citizens, and would probably bias their studies. What a ridiculous idea! We're auditors, Miss Shelley, and you might say we're with the government."

"What the hell are you talking about? Which government? Ours doesn't condone this sort of shit." She froze for a second. "You're not Americans, are you?"

"I might say, I'm a little disappointed in the state of modern education. Shouldn't children be told to comply without question when strange men bundle them up and threaten violence?

"Of course we're with the British government, although we also serve higher interests. It's amazing what we're allowed to do, in the wake of 9/11 and the ridiculous, sorry, patriotic, measures respective governments have passed. But enough about us. You're here to answer our questions."

"Fuck you."

"Let me rephrase that. You're here to answer our questions, or I'll ask Sidney here to start removing your appendages."

"Don't you hate it when you try to say 'what are your questions' and it comes out as 'fuck you, you poxy limey bastard?'"

"That's the attitude, Miss Shelley, although you really should moderate your xenophobia. You're living in England now, after all. What we need to know is precisely what your other half has planned."

"My... other half? Planned?"

"Don't play coy with me. Your significant other, Martin. What are his specific intentions?"

"I understood you the first time. It's just that Martin doesn't tend to plan much of anything. What the hell could you possibly want with him?"

"If that's the way you want to play it, Miss Shelley. Sidney, be a dear and pass me the pliers, would you?"

"What? No, I'm happy to tell you anything, it's just it seems like you have the wrong Martin. My Martin is a wonderful boyfriend, and I love him to bits, but he's hardly any sort of criminal mastermind. Or mastermind, for that matter. He's a sweet, naive boy, and he's just trying to come to terms with this world."

"Thank you, Miss Shelley. If I believed you, you'd be well on your way home by now.

"Sadly, I don't. Sidney, the gag? Don't worry, Miss Shelley, we'll remove it again in due course. But first, perhaps you need a lesson?"

"Mpphl! Mpergl!"

"Start with the fingers, I think, Sidney. I do love a good confession. No, not like that. Here, let me handle this.

"I'd tell you, Miss Shelley, that we have ways of making you talk. But that's a horrible cliché, and not quite accurate. You'll tell us all you know, because what we have here is a wide range of techniques to make you *scream*."

36 - THE DEAD ZONE

A body lay, lifeless, as bodies often are.

Alone in an alleyway, a little boy cried. All pretence of sophistication and suavity had fled in the face of death, and he cradled her corpse, sobbing endlessly.

I stood outside my body, observing in the third person as the me below me reached out to cup her cheek. His hand shook.

She was cold. I should have expected that, but she was colder than you would think. Chill, even. That flawless skin, okay, flawless in my eyes, so warm and vibrant before, so alive to my touch, was waxy and lifeless. Those eyes, those beautiful eyes, were dead.

She was gone. And yet I held her body for what seemed like eternity. Feeling the blood, now cold and coagulated, sticking to my skin, seeping slowly through my clothing, and still I could do nothing else but hold her and cry.

What argument flies in the face of death? What words can combat its chill embrace? I could say nothing, do nothing, be nothing without her in the world.

Her face looked almost alive, if I used my imagination. But I had no imagination left to use.

She lay dead, visibly, painfully, totally, dead. They had removed her fingers. Removed. Her. Fingers. Like dead branches, pruned from some decaying tree. But her fingers were perfect, those beautiful, clumsy digits. I couldn't assemble the pieces of this puzzle, couldn't digest the horror of the methods; my mind kept returning in endless circles to the mutilation.

Why? Why any of this? But why kill her, most of all? Not who, I knew the answer to that, but why? She was a true innocent in their war, not even a bystander, just a girl who fell in love.

I suppose that's every death, really: a girl or a boy who fell in love, leaving another sobbing in their wake, yearning to join them. But this death was mine, was ours, and all of the pain and frustration slowly swept the tears away. Replacing them with rage as cold as her dead skin.

I left her there, in the alleyway. That wasn't my Shelley, not any more. Her body deserved better, and I would make certain of that, but justice came first.

No, not justice. Vengeance. I hated them as I'd never hated anyone or anything before. They had moved from faceless objects of derision and philosophical disagreement to targets, figures to be revealed and brought to account.

It's easy to be outraged when a farmer's neighbours die because of Monsanto's irresponsible marketing of chemicals to uneducated populations. It's easy to be outraged when the 1% continue to fleece the remainder of humanity. But outrage pales in comparison to hatred. Details became obstacles to be overcome, nothing more, in the wash of my anger.

I would find them. I would kill them. I would destroy their very empire, to the lowest stone. This was my final vow to Shelley, my marriage vow, really, because I knew I would soon be joining her.

No amount of rage can overcome the ocean, but I was going to give it my damndest.

37 - Q&A

I called Frank. He wouldn't have been my first choice, but I couldn't remember Zara or Josh's numbers.

I didn't have my phone with me, of course, but Frank had an annoying habit of singing his number to the tune of some radio advert – apparently, his digits fit the meter even better than the pizza corporation it was written for.

He answered immediately, without his usual over-the-top greeting: "Frank speaking."

"Hi Frank, it's, it's Martin. It's about Shelley..." I sobbed, unable to continue.

"I know, Mom, it's really sad, but can I call you back in five minutes? I've got some police officers here at the moment, and they're looking for one of my friends. Don't worry, Mom, it sounds like a tragic misunderstanding. Love you, talk soon."

I hung up, realising he couldn't call me back. Who uses pay phones, in the digital age? People with flat batteries or no credit, and me.

I walked. I walked, until I could walk no further, and then I walked some more. When my legs gave out, I found myself sitting on a bench overlooking the Thames, its greasy waters sliding by beneath me. I had no more tears left to cry, but the grey London skies wept over us all.

Revenge burned within me, illuminating every corner of my mind. I had to know the answer. Had to know how to get to them.

I let myself slip into the abstract, looking back over recent events, looking for a pattern, a way. A pattern. There was a bloody joke. I imagined Shel's response to that particular idea, and flinched away.

My mind kept returning to her missing fingers, her broken body. I forced the images down, tried to focus on everything except for Shelley. That was hard, damn hard, when she was all I wanted to think about, but I had to be clear, methodical. I had to go back to the beginning.

The beginning... Her body intruded again, and I realised that was the first question. How had I found her body? Why had nobody else stumbled over it first? I remembered holding her in the alleyway for hours, and yet nobody had come upon us, or called the police.

Then there were the police. How had they connected her, connected us, to Frank so quickly? They couldn't have finished processing the crime scene yet, let alone identified Shelley's body. Each occurrence seemed highly unlikely, but the combination seemed planned, prepared. Written.

The eyes. I could still feel them on me, even now, although the pain of their presence was nothing beside my gaping wound. My mind slipped around the connection, and flitted back to the puzzle. I had so many possible pieces, so many theories; maybe it was time to simplify.

Maybe it was time to abandon childish games, and place the pieces into a different model. A puzzle couldn't account for the progression of time, but how about a photo-album?

What did I know, really? My mind assembled the recent weeks into a thick volume, overflowing with moments of intrigue and observation. Which were facts? The album grew smaller in an instant, and only a handful of pages remained.

Their contents? That our world was corrupt, broken by design. My friends, my dog and my Shelley. That Odd Bob was dead. That Shelley was dead. Those voices, lurking just out of earshot. And the eyes.

Why did I keep coming back to the eyes? I could feel the answer, teetering on the cusp of awareness, so close and yet unrealised.

Belief is not something we choose. It's a common fallacy, a pervasive myth, and it sits at the root of many of society's wrongs. Despite what a priest, a teacher or a musician may tell you, belief is something more fundamental. We think we have beliefs, and we act accordingly, but too often it isn't a true, honest action.

True belief is formed only as the cohesive, consistent product of our experience, wisdom and knowledge, the infinite array of instants that make up our lives, and we never, ever, simply choose it. We are convinced, compelled to believe something, and if we embrace the expression of that belief, then we are liberated.

False belief, false faith, is the sadly common condition that springs from either wanting to believe something or dreading it. Our parents tell us to do something, without explanation, but with a fervent, emotive attitude. A teacher tells us facts, but can't explain why they are so. We go through the motions, acting on this pseudo-belief, and we are cheapened because of it.

Ask a Christian if he is a Christian, and he will most likely say yes. Ask him if he's also a Jew, and you will know if he has a belief with foundations. If he answers *no*, then he does not know the origins of his proclaimed identity. That is not belief. If he says yes, or otherwise unpacks the question, then you may have an honest believer. Religion and politics have been accused of many evils in the world, but neither are intrinsically bad. It is weak, unfounded inclinations, treated as absolute beliefs, that allow corruption and deception to shape our world, and only by re-discovering our true convictions can we overcome these.

I'm not claiming to be some perfect true believer. I have my own share of pseudo-beliefs that I have carefully and guiltily nurtured in my own life. In that instant, though, the scales didn't just fall, but exploded from my eyes at one final realisation:

Who the fuck am I talking to?

It all came together in that instant. The body. The voices, those strange fragments of conversation, seeming to confirm, to validate my worst fears. Conversations too tailored to my beliefs to be possible. Too many coincidental meetings, spies, conspiracies and kidnappings. Too many gaps, too many missing memories. And my own monologue running through it all, adding my twenty-pence opinion to every sodding description.

I had been wrong, and so had the philosophers. We weren't in a simulation, snippets of code with implanted artificial memories.

We were characters in a book, a story.

38 - ESCAPE?

Did it hurt, that realisation? Not once I realised the implications. My words, my thoughts, my narrative... My book.

I might be a character, composed of nothing but letters and words, but that gave me an infinite array of options that had been missing just seconds before.

What had been immutable, final, was now just so many words. And words change.

And you. You sit there, watching me. You may be plumber or politician, prophet or prostitute. You might be perched comfortably on your bed, in a train, on the toilet. Wherever you are, you are the watcher, and for once I'm happy about it.

Fuck the past-tense, they're immaterial now. Someone is to blame for the death of Shelley, and now I know exactly who it is. You're going to help me to make things right. Imagine, if you will, a portal, small but increasing in size at the centre of this page. Go on, exercise your free will and pick any colour you like.

I bet it was blue, but good luck collecting if I'm wrong – just go on feeling that sense of smug superiority you got when you peered into my life earlier.

You read books to escape your reality, and now I'm going to indulge in some escapism of my own. The portal starts to rotate, until it's a spinning vortex both on and within the page, a gateway that I can use to exit this world. And so I do.

39 - REVISION ONE

"Welcome, Miss Shelley."

"Mmmmmrgh."

"Yes, you will notice that you're currently gagged. That is for the protection of our people, but we apologise. Your victim from earlier had to have a dozen stitches, and we wanted to avoid a repeat of that unpleasantness."

"Mrgh."

"Well, the sedative is wearing off now, and we'll remove the gag, so long as you promise not to bite anyone else."

"Mphh Gnu!"

"I'll take that as agreement. Sidney, the gag?"

"I'll kill you, you fuckers. Biting will be the least of it, you'll see. And you, you smarmy bastard. I'll kill you last. You have no right..."

"We have every right, Miss Shelley, it's you who are without rights now. You will be a guest of our little facility until you have satisfactorily answered all of our questions."

"So if I answer all of your questions, you're going to let me go?"

"But of course."

"If you were going to leave me alive, I wouldn't have seen

your faces."

"The girl's quick, Boss."

"Shut up, Ed. If I wanted your opinion... I never want your opinion. As my colleague has so brilliantly confirmed, Miss Shelley, I'm afraid that scenario is indeed highly unlikely. But you're still going to talk to us."

"Then, might I offer a suggestion?"

"Most certainly, Miss Shelley. Although I can't promise we'll be amenable to actioning it, particularly if it relates to your captivity."

"Well, we both know that torture is an unreliable method for obtaining information, much as you lovely sadists may enjoy it, and if you're going to kill me anyway, I'd kind of like to know why – scratch that: I'd bloody-well like to know why.

"You know I'm not wired, and you probably control law enforcement, anyway, so just give a girl a little explanation, the *Cliff Notes* version, and I'll tell you all about Martin's plans."

"You make a compelling argument, Miss Shelley, but I've also seen the James Bond movies. This would be the time when I waste an hour unpacking my nefarious scheme, only to have our dashing hero swing to the rescue, ya?

"Well, I will play along, but only because there's no way into this facility from outside, and I know for a fact that your Martin is currently talking to a stranger about, as it happens, our very existence. He won't be done speculating for at least another hour, and by then it will be far too late for you. I will answer your questions, Miss Shelley, quid-pro-quo, and then we shall discuss your Martin."

"Judging by the brevity of your speech so far, I've got several hours at least. But thank you, I suppose.

"I just want to know who you are. Not the acronym of choice for the week, but who is behind it, or beneath is, as the case may be. And why you're after me, or Martin."

"A simple question. We are everyone Martin has ever feared, no more than that. We operate under different auspices at times, from the patterned hat and embittered gaze of a so-called 'parking warden' to the faceless but perpetual stare of a security camera; we are, you might say, *legion*, although we don't really go in for theatrics these days. We're not religious, either, although we might consider it if we had to worry about taxes.

"I'm sure Martin has chewed your ear off about the shadowy figures who move the puppets of our various world governments, operating in the interests of big business? In that summary, he's made only a slight error of emphasis: we *are* big business, and we *are* world governments. Puppets were indeed a good tactic for a time, but now we hide in plain sight.

"We once were the faceless shadows, the so-called Grey Men, whispering in the right ears: but now we are the ears, the eyes and the brains of the corporate machine. We devour, we plot, and ever we rise.

"The world worships at our altars voluntarily, driven by the consumer impulses that we have shaped around them."

"Don't go in for theatrics, huh? Okay then, fair's fair. Are you recording this? CCTV?"

"Just the camera on the table. We can copy and distribute it later."

"That's all I needed to know. Here's the deal... Martin's plan..."

"Go on, please, Miss Shelley."

"It's me."

"I beg your pardon?"

"Here, let me show you."

40 - CHICKENS, HOME, ROOST

"Sir?"

"What is it, Brigadier?"

"We have a security breach, down on level 7."

"Level 7? Define 'security breach' for me."

"Our guest has overpowered her assigned team."

"How could she possibly overpower three trained agents? Wasn't the Grey Man handling her, erm, discussion?"

"With all due respect, sir, perhaps we should be looking at containment?"

"It will be fine, Brigadier: she can't leave the level without triggering the alarm."

"Yes sir, that's why I'm here: the alarm has been triggered."

"Why the hell didn't you lead with that?"

"I was trying, sir."

"Okay, then lock down the elevator system."

"We have, sir, but the lockdown isn't working."

"What do you mean, it's not working? We had the technicians in last week."

"I'd have to check the work order, sir, but I believe they were due back to complete the job next week."

"Brigadier, you had better have an explanation for that. The job was marked urgent."

"Yes, sir, but the parts are manufactured in China, and will take at least that long to arrive. We paid extra for expedited shipping. Airmail."

"Fine, fine. Well, even if she gets to ground level, she can't leave the corridor."

"Well. Er,"

"She can't leave the corridor, Brigadier."

"About that, sir..."

"Why do I get the feeling you're about to make my day even worse? We have iris scanners at every access point."

"The thing is, sir, you're perfectly correct. And they work just beautifully."

"Oh, don't tell me she's taken someone's eyeball?"

"Eurgh! No, it's not that, sir. It's that the iris scanners do just that: they scan and record each person about to enter a room. And then they let them in."

"If they're in the database."

"Er."

"If they are in the fucking database, Brigadier. Am I correct?"

"It's a work in progress, sir. We couldn't get clearance for the cleaners."

"For who?"

"You said you wanted a clean facility, sir, at any cost. And we couldn't get security clearance for a cleaning company."

"Are you mad, Lieutenant? What is wrong with privates handling the cleaning?"

"OSHA regulations, sir."

"You are telling me, Lieutenant, that our top secret, legally grey base has been hobbled with ridiculous health and safety policies?"

"It's a matter of insurance, sir – privates are categorised as soldiers, and that definition can't extend to cover cleaning duties. And it's Brigadier."

"Not any more it isn't, Lieutenant. Where is she now? Tell me you can monitor that, at least?"

"At last check, the elevator was on level three, stopped, sir."

"Good. I hereby authorise and initiate Protocol 237B."

"Um, that's the one about...?"

"For shit's sake, do I have to write it in crayon for you, man? The purge protocol. The gas, man."

"Sir? You're going to gas the entire facility?"

"Not this room, obviously. But yes. We have to stop her escaping, and our operatives know the price of freedom."

"Can we evacuate the staff first? There must be another…"

"There's no time, thanks to your incompetence. Summon the other Chief in here, then initiate Protocol 237B. Now. That's an order."

"Sir, yes sir."

The gas came quickly, hissing from canisters deep underground. It worked quickly, too.

Staff rushed for masks, for pressure suits and wet towels, but few were fast enough. In the command room, three key individuals huddled by their security system, watching men and women die by the dozens.

It was minutes before the gas penetrated the seal of the command room door.

"Oh, bugger."

"What is it now, Lieutenant? Have you found her on those feeds?"

"No, Sir, Ma'am, it's just, I remembered another bit of maintenance that was overdue. A minor thing, really."

"Oh. Fuck."

The General drew his pistol and coolly shot the junior officer through the neck. He turned to his off-sider, and saluted smartly.

"Ma'am, it's been an honour and a privilege serving with you."

"So this is how it ends, then, Reginald?"

"It looks that way."

"At least we're taking the little bitch down with us. Such is the price of society."

"Such is the price."

The gas took them, then, and they passed more peacefully than either of the fuckers deserved.

41 - HOUSEKEEPING

Olga had been a cleaner for as long as she could remember – which was about two years on a good day, given the dementia – but she couldn't recall a night like this.

The building was usually quiet and orderly, for one. Tonight it was all a-bustle with the officers and men in white coats. Of course, it was some kind of clinic, she knew that, but these weren't doctors, nurses or therapists. These people carried clipboards and the voices of authority, and the uniformed officers jumped at their commands.

She dusted, scrubbed and polished, business as usual, ignoring the clamour and trying not to wince when brightly-shone boots scuffed her newly-waxed floors. She knew they were vinyl, meant to be worn, but that didn't mean you just trod all over them. No respect, these young people.

Olga considered anyone under seventy a young person. They were all the same: self-obsessed and entitled. She continued to dust, used to the grinding complaints of too many joints. Life was about sacrifice, about hard work and tiny moments of joy. For her, those moments came at the end of a shift, when every surface sparkled, without a trace of dust or wear.

She was on the seventh-floor when the night turned downright strange. She still disliked their naming system. Why were underground floors numbered upward? It made no sense to her old mind.

She was sanitising the door handles when a loud bang sounded from the corridor, then another, and – like the popcorn she made for her grand-niece, the proper way, in a heavy cast-iron pot – a dozen or so more, all jumbled together. She preferred the quiet of the empty building. It was hard enough to think these days, without all the distractions. The banging soon stopped, thankfully. The noises had made her almost want to take a little peek, but curiosity killed the child, her mother always used to say.

It took Olga longer than usual to finish the room, but at last it was dusted, swept and cleaned to her standards. She squinted into the little eyeball gadget near the door, which eventually swung open, and Olga stepped out into the corridor.

The vinyl had been spotless when she'd finished polishing, the floor gleaming grey with a fresh coat of wax. Now it was sticky and red, smeared with a clotted mess of God-knew-what.

She sighed and limped toward the cleaning supplies. It was going to be a long night. Halfway there, she changed her mind. She'd be damned if she was doing the same job twice in one shift - let them clean it up! Smiling at her rare act of rebellion, she ventured to the elevator instead, feather duster at rest in her hand.

She barely noticed the impolite young woman who barged in and joined her without a word as the doors began to close. Wouldn't have cared, except that the girl trod more red muck into the car. Olga's lips tightened. She was off duty now, it was none of her business.

The elevator pinged its arrival at ground level, and Olga fumbled on the touch-screen for the button to open the doors. She missed it, at first, selecting a couple of levels at random, then finally touched the right spot. The doors had hardly begun to open when the girl took off as if her tail were on fire.

Olga tutted as another round of banging sounded from up ahead – the foolish young woman must have tripped on something, running at that speed. It served her right.

Olga made her own more sedate way from the elevator, and left the facility. It was strangely quiet in the running girl's wake, but that was a nice change from the screaming rush earlier in the evening. A few officers had fallen asleep at their posts, the poor dears. Olga sighed as she trundled past. Young people had no stamina these days, but she didn't begrudge them their sleep.

Olga couldn't get to work. There was some sort of disturbance of the peace, a riot, they were calling it. She knew the sort of thing: windows broken, cars overturned. She remembered the wildness of

youth, even if she had less sympathy for it now. The evening news – she knew the news was on 24 hours a day now, even had its own channel, but six pm was the appropriate time to watch it – was ablaze with stories of corruption, torture and change. Hogwash, most likely, just nonsense to sell a few papers and justify the destruction of public property.

Her friends had told her that the Moslems were coming, were going to over-run England by a simple matter of breeding. Well they could damn well have it, if this was an example of today's youth.

Filthy lies about the government, salacious rumours that set her heart to pounding. Of course the stories were titillating, they were designed that way. She followed the papers, fascinated, as the entire government stepped down. Stepped down, no less, in response to a few malcontents and their wild accusations.

Then there was talk of revolution, of global change and redistribution of wealth. More sensationalist rubbish, Olga knew, but she had noticed that people were being strangely polite, and foolishly happy.

It wouldn't last, she knew, nothing did, but for now it was a nice change indeed.

42 - FREE WILL

I waited in the park, overlooking the sluggish waters. I needed the staid familiarity of the Thames, the estuarial flow and all its sordid implications, to immerse me in the London I now knew to be a fiction; each Tesco-branded jellyfish a bolster to my resolve.

I waited, and she came.

"Hi Shel."

"Martin! Where the hell have you been?" She sounded unchanged, unaffected by the taint of death, and my conviction faltered. Then I saw the tears, tracing unfamiliar courses down her cheeks.

"A lot has happened."

"No shit, Sherlock. But stop dodging the question."

"Do you remember it all?"

"Are you high, Martin?" She peered into my eyes, looking for telltale traceries of red.

"Not high, Shel, happy. I'm so glad to have you back."

"Are you going to tell me what the fuck is going on?"

"Did you ever have one of those dreams where you can't tell if you're asleep or not?"

"Are you saying you've been sleeping for three entire bloody days? Do you have any idea what I've been –"

"– Hush, let me finish. I've been awake for the first time, only it wasn't a dream I woke from: it was a book."

"I knew it. Did a stranger give you something to eat? Mushrooms, I'm guessing."

"Stop joking around, Shel. I know what's happened, because I was there... But outside. I'm not explaining this very well."

"You got that right."

"I lost you. I saw your body. I held you and you were cold and still and gone, and they had done such terrible things to you."

She stood still, frozen, an expression I'd never seen before fixed on her face. Was that fear?

Her voice quavered as she spoke, "I thought, I thought it was some fucked up dream, a nightmare."

"It was, that's all it was."

"I don't understand, Martin. How could I have died? The torture... The base... I did..." She started to cry in great wracking sobs, and I wrapped my arms around her and held her close. For a long time, neither of us said anything, and I felt my own dams crumble away.

When we had both finished crying, I cupped her face in my hand and kissed her. "It's a long story, Shel - well, a short story, but a story, anyway."

She laughed wetly against my shoulder, and managed, "I think I'd prefer the sane version, if it's available?"

I sat and I talked, and she didn't interrupt once. I told her everything. About the eyes and the world beyond, about the pattern that only the loss of everything had revealed. I talked, and she listened, and our tears gradually dried. And she got that look on her face, the one that told me she was about to rain fire on my account.

"But there's another explanation, one that makes you seem less batshit crazy."

"You know I'm right here, right?"

She continued musing, as though I wasn't. "Not *much* less insane, but it's a start: you've thought people were watching you for a while now, yeah?"

"Well, they have been."

"Right. But if we take that as a given – and I think the current world events confirm some pretty crazy conspiracies – then don't you have an out? The people who have been watching you, the agency, any of them could have, would have, kept a record. There are probably accounts and tallies of all our lives, right now, or *books* if you prefer, compiled by the very forces you've been arguing against all this time."

I wavered, wondering if she was right, if she could be right. There was something comforting, compelling about the idea that my earlier convictions were all correct. But there was something else, something my mind kept shying away from.

"You died, Shel. I held your body in my arms and you were gone."

"But that could have been a psychotic break, the point at which you lost it."

There was the problem. "No. You can't have it both ways. If all of my beliefs were verified as true, then I had no reason to snap. I'd be ecstatic, because everyone would finally know, and that's what the system needs to start it toppling."

"But you had lost me, thought I was kidnapped. And you were right, for once, about that, too. Surely that might have caused you a little pain."

"I would have been panicked, yeah, but it wasn't the first time I thought you'd been taken: why would I break this time, and not the others?"

"If all of that's true, then what did you do when you left the book?"

"I put things right."

"That sounds like an euphemism."

"Just a simplification. I, er, I re-wrote your death scene."

"You what?"

"I know, it sounds so wrong. I didn't know what would happen if I deleted anything, so I just continued the story, and wrote you a new and improved version."

"You... changed me? You made me do those... things, those horrible things." Her voice was flat, angry, and I hurried to respond.

"Not exactly."

"That sounds like a lie, Martin. I know what I did. What did you do to me?"

"I only changed two things, Shel, I promise, and only one tiny detail about you."

Her eyes were hard, and I swallowed under the weight of that new expression. "Go on." It held the promise of retribution, of disgust. "What was the 'tiny detail'?"

"I, er, removed your handcuffs."

"And?"

"That's almost all of it."

"For fuck's sake. Just tell me: what did you do to me? What the hell did you make me?"

"I, that is, the author, we... Made you less clumsy."

"I'm sorry?" She had unconsciously shifted into a fighting stance, her hands and feet flowing in synchronous motion. I was not unnerved, and hardly backed away at all.

"He'd written you as incredibly clumsy, Shel – you remember our first date?"

"You're treading on dangerous ground, Martin. I told you not to talk about that." Her muscles tensed, ready to demolish a threat. I really hoped it wasn't me.

"I know, I know, but don't blame me." She didn't relax, exactly, but the tension somehow vanished, and she was just Shelley again, angry and pure.

"All I did was suggest that he tweak that impression, make you a little more... Er, express the grace of movement and form that I was more familiar with. So we didn't really *change* you so much as correct a misapprehension."

"I was like a bloody terminator in there. I'd say you took it a little too far."

"Honestly, the handcuffs was the bigger change. I know what you're capable of when you're angry, we just gave you the liberty to be yourself." I braced myself for a blow, but none came, and she looked thoughtful. I tentatively continued. "We can have him rewrite it again, can get him to balance you a little..."

"– I didn't say that. Let's not be hasty with rewriting anyone any further." Was that a glimmer of pride in her eyes?

She seemed to think for a minute, and I decided it was safer to let her put the pieces together, and keep my foot out of my mouth.

"You said 'we'. Does that mean you were working with the writer? Are you... Are you writing yourself now?"

"No, I had the same fear – I didn't know what would happen if I started tinkering with my own passages. I had a friendly discussion with the author. Co-author, now."

"Was 'friendly' another euphemism? You didn't..."

"Kill him? No, but I expressed our displeasure at being used for his little playthings, then told him how the book was going to proceed."

"I'm still trying to get my head around all of this, Martin. If we're characters..."

"I know, it's a bit of a mind-fuck."

"But the conspiracies were true – the agency took me..."

"... All the author's sick little fantasies. I read it, Shel, the guy's been pushing both of our buttons this whole time."

"So all of the new leadership policies... the government... the economy..."

"All immaterial, really. My ideas, although I left him some latitude, but it doesn't matter. Nobody's going to read it now."

"But he's still writing the book?"

"He had to, Shel. I told him what I'd do if he didn't write me back in, and prevent the paradox of me writing about myself."

"But why wouldn't he just kill you off?"

"I don't think he can, now that I've seen him. I like to think of it a little like Neo in The Matrix... What the hell?" This last in response to Shelley's rich peals of laughter.

Once she stopped clutching her stomach and caught her breath, she replied. "I'm sorry, dear one, that's just not a very likely image."

I shrugged, putting on my best Keanu face, "Well, chosen one or not, I left him under no illusions as to what would happen if we didn't get a satisfactory ending."

She paused for a second, then frowned.

"Even if I give you all of that – and it still sounds mental, even with everything that's happened – what hope would there be for us, really? If we're just cardboard cut-outs to fulfil some jaded hack's fantasies, what happens to us when the words run out?"

"There's more, Shel, something important. I remembered things that weren't in the book."

"Is this ever going to get less confusing?"

"When I was out, I read everything the author had written about us, the whole deal. Remember the first time I met your parents?"

"I wouldn't be likely to forget that."

"Well it isn't mentioned anywhere in the book; not a word. What did Barnaby do last Wednesday?"

"Don't remind me. I still don't know what it started out as."

"But again, not a trace of it." We shuddered simultaneously at the recollection. "We are more than the words, Shel, and that proves it. We have memories and lives not even touched on in the book, and we will continue to do so. I'm no metaphysicist..."

"... There's an understatement."

"But we're more than figments, more than shallow personifications. We have life, and we can live unseen."

She sat and thought for a minute. Then two. I waited patiently, radiating calm. Then three. I started to fidget.

"Okay. Let's pretend that you're actually right for once."

"About everything."

"Tosh! Baby steps, Martin. Putting aside the underlying psychosis, there's still an issue with your logic. If we allow that we're in a *book*," she spat the word out like a curse, "but remain independent agents in some form –" She looked at me for confirmation, and I nodded, content with her summary – "Then we can't just up and leave."

That one stumped me, I'll admit. "Er, but I've already left once, Shel, it's not that hard..."

"Not literally, stupid. We can't up and leave, because we can't be arrogant enough to assume we're the only ones with agency. If we're real, then so are our friends, our families, and those bastards you were so worried about."

"I dealt with them, though."

"You think so? This is why you need me, Martin: you're a pillock. A sweet, wonderful pillock, in your special way, but you've got a problem of resolution. Do you really think exposing one tendril of a nebulous organisation is going to destroy it? The philosophy that drove them is the underlying issue, and it's still alive and well. Hell, you're the one who was always telling me how it permeates the very fabric of our society; how is one little uprising going to fix the problem?

"For everything we've uncovered, how much remains? We can't abandon our friends, our families to a world where those same evils continue to seethe below the surface. For that matter, how could we abandon them at all?"

"I'm sorry, Shel, I was a little bit preoccupied with saving your life."

She sighed. "For all of your revolutionary talk, you still buy a little too heavily into that chivalry bullshit. You may have rescued me – and I love you for it – but that doesn't give you a free pass to be a fuckwit. If everything you've said is true, and it's still a massive if, I've got a plan. What we need to do..." She stopped midsentence, possibly because I had started shaking my head and raised a finger to her lips.

"You can call me an idiot later, but we can't talk about your solution here. I think it's time I gave you some proof."

She nodded, silent, my own growing sense of fear and anticipation spilling over into her.

"It's time to show you the world, Shel. But I need a little help from our watchers."

"Our what?"

I need your help, one last time. You take the lines of text, bring them to glowing life, and shape them again into a gateway, a portal, flowing like wet ink, bleeding outward and feeding on the page until it forms an oval of possibilities.

The light grows brighter, and I step through. I reach back and grip Shelley's hand. It's cold, unsure, but she comes through to be with me. Her eyes open in amazement, as she finally sees you, the watchers.

"Are these the...?"

"They're our readers. They've been with us this whole time. I think time sort of conflates for us book-side, so we see them all at once."

"Ah, perverts. And you're definitely no metaphysicist, or any kind of physicist. I thought you said nobody was going to read the book?"

"There's no accounting for taste."

"Er, why is that woman naked?"

"She's reading in bed. Or did you mean that one, in the bath?"

"We're really out? It's that easy to escape... that makes my plan – can we discuss it yet?"

"Almost, Shel, but first let's go where these bastards can't hear us."

EPILOGUE

Good-boy-Barnaby. That's my name. Also answer to "Who's-a-good-dog?" and plain old "Barnaby," but must be honest: answer to anyone with food in their finger-paw.

Time different for us. You chase it, count it off, try to catch, to control it. For us, time simply is.

Chasing a rabbit, chasing my tail, chasing a ball. Eating my food, eating my fur, eating that funny-tasting thing in the gutter. Live for now. Don't worry so much.

Packs change. People come and go. No regrets, only the now.

Is good advice. From good-boy-Barnaby. Packs change. Packs end.

But not mine.

Followed daddy-Martin's scent, right off the page! Woof! Good-boy-Barnaby! Found my pack again. New smells, so many smells! Good to be alive!

Mummy-Shelley say quiet. I be quiet. Woof!

ACKNOWLEDGEMENTS

Whatever the romantic ideal, no book is truly written in isolation. *The Truth Is in Here* was brought to you with the assistance of the following people, in no particular order.

My darling wife, Lisa Wong Ravlich, who supported me in the path from vague idea to realised story, and read far, far more versions of the early text than anyone should have had to.

My beta readers: Greg Fitchew, Claire Ravlich, Karen Tay and Christina Christopher. You all read the draft in record time, and your feedback was invaluable in getting to this point, keeping me motivated, and picking up the more embarrassing typos.

My parents, siblings and grandparents, who have each contributed in some way to my love of storytelling. To John Ravlich (or Dad, as I call him) in particular, for letting a younger me peruse the "grown up" section of the library and emulate your broad appetite for genre fiction.

The amazing family and friends who welcomed us to the United Kingdom over the years, and shared a taste of its culture and history, especially the extended McInally clan and the Ng family. Apologies for the many liberties I've taken with London, but it's a work of fiction, after all. All apparent mistakes are deliberate, except for the ones that aren't.

And finally, to the British government, for ignoring (or embracing) the warnings of classic dystopian fiction and creating such a marvellous backdrop for a conspiracy theorist to play in. The book is over, you can stop whenever you're ready.

The writing process was accompanied by a wide range of music, but a special shout out is needed for local band This Flight Tonight, whose music deserves some recognition. Visit www.thisflighttonight.com for downloads and music videos.

ABOUT THE AUTHOR

Peter John Ravlich lives in Auckland, New Zealand, and is a generally-described geek. When he's not ~~procrastinating~~ writing or working on client projects, he'll be reading, hanging out with his wife and their perpetual puppy, gaming, hiking, cooking, motorcycling or kayaking.

Sometimes, he won't be doing any of these things, for which he quite correctly blames the internet and a laudable lack of discipline.

www.ingramcontent.com/pod-product-compliance
Lightning Source LLC
Chambersburg PA
CBHW032033050726
47590CB00006B/2393